FLAWLESS GIRLS

FLAWLESS GIRLS

GIRLS

ANNA-MARIE McLEMORE

FEIWEL AND FRIENDS
NEW YORK

A Feiwel and Friends Book
An imprint of Macmillan Publishing Group, LLC
120 Broadway, New York, NY 10271 • fiercereads.com

Our books may be purchased in bulk for promotional, educational,
or business use. Please contact your local bookseller or the Macmillan
Corporate and Premium Sales Department at (800) 221-7945 ext. 5442 or by
email at MacmillanSpecialMarkets@macmillan.com.

Library of Congress Cataloging-in-Publication Data

Names: McLemore, Anna-Marie, author.
Title: Flawless girls / Anna-Marie McLemore.
Description: First edition. | New York : Feiwel and Friends, 2024. |
    Audience: Ages 13-18. | Audience: Grades 10-12. | Summary: "After
    her sister goes missing, Isla Soler re-enrolls at the opulent Alarie
    House, intent on finding out what happened to her"— Provided
    by publisher.
Identifiers: LCCN 2023046311 | ISBN 9781250869630 (hardcover)
Subjects: CYAC: Schools—Fiction. | Sisters—Fiction. | Intersex
    people—Fiction. | Hispanic Americans—Fiction.
Classification: LCC PZ7.1.M463 Fl 2024 | DDC [Fic]—dc23
LC record available at https://lccn.loc.gov/2023046311

First edition, 2024
Book design by Abby Granata
Feiwel and Friends logo designed by Filomena Tuosto
Printed in the United States of America

ISBN 978-1-250-86963-0
1 3 5 7 9 10 8 6 4 2

**In memory of Ellie and Dorothy,
two grandmothers who knew how to sparkle.**

*And while we're here, a note to the pendejo
who stole my abuela's diamond necklace:*

You know who you are.

*More to the point,
I know who you are.*

*Good little Mexican girls
notice a lot more than you think.*

FLAWLESS GIRLS

ONE

EVERY ALARIE GIRL BEGAN at the Alarie House. Before she ever appeared in the society pages, before her glamorous travels were chronicled in glossy magazine spreads, before she walked down the aisle in a cathedral-length veil to marry some prince fifteenth in line for the throne, she studied grace, charm, and etiquette. And she did so with more dedication than most trust-fund boys applied to their university courses.

For generations, the third most famous finishing school in the world—it would have been both folly and in poor taste to compete with the reputation of the Swiss—had turned out girls whose loveliness was both understated and unforgettable. They were composed but gracious, demure but lively. They laughed at just the correct volume. By instinct, they sat with their chairs exactly the right distance from the table, not so close as to risk jabbing their dining companions with their elbows, not so far that they had to lean over their plates and ruin their posture. They adorned their hair with precisely the right width of satin ribbon, or the right number of summer blossoms (fresh, never faux; any society girl knew that only harlots attended balls with hair dressed in fabric flowers). At tea, they breezily enjoyed the raspberry jam that never touched their white chiffon dresses. At evening dances, they ate madeleines covered in snowdrifts of powdered sugar without ever marring their black velvet gowns.

They learned these enchanted graces at a sprawling white stucco house, roofed with curving ceramic tiles that resembled a waving copper sea when the sun struck them. Many daughters dreamed of enrolling there as they turned the pages of magazines featuring Alarie girls' engagement soirees and philanthropic galas. Future debutantes feigned boredom at the very prospect of finishing school, while secretly hoping that they would be summoned to none other than the Alarie House. Distinguished families called in favors to secure their daughters' admission. There were no applications. Direct inquiries were so vulgar as to warrant disqualification. The campus was walled and hidden behind flanks of cypress trees, tall and richly green, and there was no path in except to know the right people, who knew the right people, who could tactfully recommend a name.

The Soler sisters had a grandmother who knew just enough of the right people.

TWO

ISLA AND RENATA SOLER'S grandmother had raised them to be brazen. To speak up if a man had gotten a fact wrong and they knew it. To wear whatever colors they favored even if they were out of fashion, to wear trousers to tea if they liked (provided the pair was tailored and pressed).

But their abuela also knew that two girls born with brown skin and raised by a brash businesswoman would be held to more exacting standards than their paler, more demure counterparts. The Alarie imprimatur could only help them. It could only ease their way in life, she told them. *If those women think well of you, no one will dare say a word against you. Whatever they think of a girl, whatever they think of her family, it's as good as law.*

Abuela did not say the rest. She did not need to. If Renata and Isla were Alarie girls, the society ladies could slight them only at their own peril. La plata heredada, the old money families who sneered at Abuela's fresh green wealth, would have to keep their sneers to themselves.

Their first evening at the Alarie House, older sister Renata was already showing promise. At dinner, she seemed at home among the more experienced girls, all of them cool as a breeze from a lavender field.

But just shy of midnight, younger sister Isla burst into their shared room. She did so without discretion, decorum, or composure. She was frenzied as a small storm.

Her dark hair was disarrayed. Her dark eyes looked freckled with light, as though they reflected, all at once, every jewel set into the walls of the Alarie House.

The damp rasping of Isla's breathing jostled Renata halfway from sleep. Before she could fall back under, Isla shook her shoulder and whispered, "We have to get out of here."

Renata sat up in bed, shoulders straight, posture as gently upright as it had been at the dinner table. But groggy confusion twisted her face. "What time is it?"

"Half past time to get up." Isla threw Renata's traveling coat onto her bed. The tailored burgundy velvet landed heavy, the slight puff of the upper sleeves deflating on impact. "We're leaving."

Renata blinked, her eyes adjusting to the lamp Isla had just turned on. "What are you talking about?"

"The girls here." Isla put on her own coat, identical to Renata's but dark blue. So many of Isla's clothes were slightly different copies of Renata's.

Isla slipped the coat on over her nightgown, not bothering with a dress. No one would see it anyway once she buttoned the front, and the faster they left, the better. "There's something"— even searching for the right word made her shudder—"off about them. I don't know what, but I have a bad feeling."

"You always have a bad feeling about other girls." Renata's dark curls streamed down her shoulders as though she'd been lounging in a wind-brushed field. But her face was a little paler, as it always was in the middle of the night. Even her violet nightgown seemed paler, almost lavender. "Georgette's one of the few people in the world besides Abuela and me who you can stand to listen to at a stretch. But when you first met her, you thought she was a prude."

"She always had her head tilted to the side like a statue of la Virgen." Isla threw things into her bag by the unruly handful. "I didn't know she does that without realizing it. I thought she was posing."

"You decided Yvaine was a snob within minutes of meeting her."

"It was the way she scrunched up her nose."

"It was spring." Renata drew her graceful legs out from under the blankets. "She's allergic to pollen."

"I know that now." Isla kicked a pair of shoes toward Renata. If Renata really meant to continue this argument, they'd have to save it for the train. "And anyway, she would've been right to be a snob. The dress I was wearing when you first introduced me to her, who would have blamed her? I still can't believe you let me go out like that."

Isla thought that would at least earn her a smile.

Renata only pointed her feet and kicked at one of the shoes. It flopped over. "And you told me Rosine wouldn't know a good comeback if it bit her in the orto."

"I didn't know her yet. Her neutral expression just looks confused. Even you have to admit that."

"Exactly. You didn't know her yet. You didn't know any of them when you first met them because, shock of great shocks, you had just met them." Renata was on her feet now. Good. One step closer to out the door. "But you wrote them off like you're writing off the girls here, before you know anything about them."

"These aren't your friends back home." Isla slipped her feet into her shoes and fastened the buckles. "The girls here, they're—" What were they? In their white dresses, fresh and flowing as sunlight, they seemed not quite real. They seemed ghostly, as though Isla might fall through one of them if she didn't watch where she was going.

None of that sounded convincing enough. And there was no time to explain what had just happened. Isla wasn't breathing a word of it until they were miles out of earshot.

A match caught in the back of Isla's brain. She didn't have to explain it.

She could show Renata.

With an anticipatory shudder, Isla threw the door open.

But there was nothing but darkness in the halls. Nothing but the low sparkle from the dimly lit chandelier.

They had all just been out there, girls lined up in their white nightgowns. Their staring faces had turned as nightmarish as they were dreamlike during the day. They had looked like a flank of dolls advancing. They had looked as though they were about to converge on Isla and do, what? Turn her nightgown white with the sheer bleaching power of their gazes? Tear her open with their perfectly buffed fingernails? Bite into her heart like an apple? Eat handfuls of her veins like the threads of a squash?

But now they had vanished.

Isla shut the door.

The confusion on Renata's face shifted into annoyance.

Isla clutched for the words to explain herself. "There's something wrong"—she stumbled even saying this—"really truly wrong, with them."

"You always think something is wrong with *them*." Renata said the word as though she meant every other girl in the world. "Did you ever think that something is wrong with *you*?"

The words fell slowly, a knife landing in half-time.

Renata's face instantly registered shock, as though she'd taken the impact of those words instead of saying them.

"I didn't mean that," she said.

Renata's words struck so gradually and with such force it was as though they had knocked into Isla's shoulder. The impact spun her around toward the door. She caught herself on the knob more than she reached for it.

"Isla," Renata whispered as loudly as whispers went.

Renata's words found their mark, deep in Isla's chest. They became a hot whirl of rage at her sister's stubbornness, and shame at how well her sister knew her, and knew her secrets.

If Isla didn't leave this house, that searing whirl would become something solid and permanent. She could feel it turning as hard as her ribs, hard as the jewels set into the Alarie House walls. If Isla didn't get out of here, it would grow facets and edges sharp enough to cut open her heart.

Isla left the room. She ran down the carpeted staircase. The gem-inlaid walls shimmered by. She threw wide the nearest door and sped down the walk. Her feet flew over the gray stone. She ran across the grounds, her shadow tiny and short compared to the tall, thin knives cast by cypress trees.

As her feet crunched over the gravel, speed filled her nightgown with chilled air. It fanned her coat out behind her like a cape. She didn't stop when the thin brushstroke of a crescent moon rose, a whisper of light in the dampening blue.

By the time the sun came up, she had already boarded the earliest train.

Isla had meant what she told Renata. There was something wrong with the girls at the Alarie House.

But Renata would find out soon what Isla had done. And no matter what Isla had told her, she would assume this was the true reason that Isla had fled.

THREE

"**YOU HAVE A WHOLE** room full of books," Isla told her grandmother. "If I need to learn which shape of glass contains which variety of wine, I'm sure one of them can tell me."

Isla knew that Abuela could hardly argue. She thought the same thing. Still, Isla could feel her grandmother holding back her questions about why she had returned from the Alarie House after a single day. And Isla kept putting off telling her the truth. She'd have to eventually. The Alarie sisters would call, outraged, after discovering what Isla had done. One of the girls must have told them by now. One of the girls must have told them before Isla had even boarded her train.

The threat was bristling in the air like an electrical storm.

Now all Isla could do was wait for it, and hope that the Alarie sisters would place the blame where it belonged, completely on her, not on Renata, not on Abuela. Which was the best strategy to get them all out of this as unscathed as possible? Should Abuela and Renata act utterly shocked? Or should Isla be painted as the rotten one of the Soler sisters, whom Abuela and Renata had so badly hoped could be transformed into a refined young lady?

It would be easy to believe, Renata succeeding where Isla had failed. Renata was the far more stunning Soler sister, tall and striking, with the highly arched eyebrows and slight smile of a girl who kept delicious secrets. Isla was so much less than Renata, in both stature and presence, that she seemed like an afterthought of a younger sister.

Perhaps if Abuela and Renata both acted as though their hopes had been dashed, the Alarie sisters would feel sorry for them, and wouldn't ruin the Soler name.

That week, an envelope arrived.

Not from the Alarie sisters, but from Renata.

> Dear Isla,
>
> I didn't mean it. You have to know I didn't mean it.
>
> Please come back. There's a reason Abuela sent us here. The Alarie name opens doors. And we both know that even if we wear

dresses straight from the atelier and read as many newspapers as Abuela, there will still be doors closed to us.

This is our chance, hermana. Let's take it.

Your sister,

R.

No mention of what Isla had done. Had none of the other girls told Renata? Had the Alarie sisters shown the decency not to hold one sister accountable for the sins of the other?

The next week brought no angry dispatches from the Alarie sisters. Just another letter from Renata.

Dear Isla,

Did you know the Alarie sisters each wear the same color all the time? Luisa, ever in blues, Alba, constantly in tints of purple, and Eduarda, eternally in hues of pale yellow.

It's not that I don't admire the state-ment of it—it's a bit like fairies in a story, isn't it? But the thing is that no one ever says anything about it, as though it's the most obvious thing in the world that a woman would wear variations on the same shade day after day. Wearing black every day I might understand, but the same Easter pastel?

As soon as I noticed it, you were the first person I wanted to tell. I wish you were here to see for yourself.

The girls here are nice enough. Really, they are, and I think you'd like them much better than you think you would. I know they'd like you. But not a one of them is you. No matter how much I enjoy their company, none of them take the sting out of not having you here.

None of them is as much fun to tell things to.

Yours,
R.

The next week brought another.

Dear Isla,

Perhaps I should have said this in my first letter:

I know why you are the way you are. I know you don't rush to judgment simply for the joy of it. I know there are reasons. I know what *happened with the other girls when you were in school. I know you think I don't know the specifics, but I listen, and I hear things Abuela says when she thinks I'm not nearby, so I know exactly what those pendejas—*

Isla threw the letter into the fireplace without reading the rest. Renata's clotted pity crawled over Isla's back like a chill, and she didn't want one more word of it.

The embers in the hearth perked to life. They spread into petals of flame and swallowed the page.

FOUR

ISLA HELD TO HER story. She considered the Alarie House a waste of time, she said. Anything she could learn there, she could learn from her grandmother, and learn to keep tidy accounting records at the same time. To prove her point, Isla became a dedicated assistant for her grandmother's paperwork, starting each morning with her correspondence.

Abuela's study was Isla's favorite room in the house. The dark wood of the shelves warmed the space, and the book spines gleamed with their titles stamped in silver and gold.

Whenever her grandmother struggled to read a particular line, she would lay it on the desk between them and they would combine Isla's sharp eyesight with Abuela's talent for deciphering scrawled or smudged handwriting.

But there was something different in how her grandmother looked down through her glasses at the letter she'd just opened.

Isla was just about to ask who it was from when she recognized the shadows of the handwriting through the thin vellum.

Abuela set down the letter and took off her glasses. "Your sister's coming home this week."

Isla gave an echoing, "Hmm."

"Apparently"—Abuela folded the page back into its original thirds—"las Señoras Alarie have deemed her polished to a shine."

Isla could feel how pinched her smile was. She tried adding a nod but could feel herself making it worse. So instead she made herself useful, picked up the teapot, and topped off her grandmother's cup. Her grandmother's "thank you, mija" was so quiet yet so crisp it sounded like the rustling of paper.

But Isla could feel her abuela watching her, each glance calibrated not to seem too curious. Her grandmother said nothing, but her unspoken questions rang in the air like the chime of a spoon against a cup.

They were probably variations on the same questions whispered in the lane. Isla may have been the lesser Soler sister, but she and Renata were a matched set, with their brightly varnished nails, unpolished shoes, and unapologetic smiles. What might a place like the Alarie House do with the older Soler girl?

And why had they done nothing with the younger one?

"I never thought you'd hate it so much," Abuela said.

Regret was so thick in her grandmother's voice that Isla could feel it, sharp as a pinch.

"I didn't hate it," Isla said. "I never said I hated it."

"It was supposed to be so good for you," Abuela said.

You.

Not *the two of you.*

Not *both of you.*

Just *you.*

In the time it took Isla's stomach to drop, the pieces sorted themselves.

This was something Abuela had wanted to give her.

"This was to teach me how to be a girl," Isla said in the same moment she thought it.

Frustration and pain vied for space in Abuela's expression. "You *are* a girl. I know that. Renata knows that. The parteras who brought you into the world know that."

The parteras who had brought Renata and Isla into the world checked on them with the diligence of godmothers, and so often they had told Isla the same thing: that she was still a girl. Even if she had a shorter, broader frame than Renata's and Abuela's graceful heights, she was still a girl. Even if she had been made differently from most girls, she was still a girl. Even if she had not developed as most girls did, did not have the same kinds of pieces to her body that most girls had, she was still a girl.

Still a girl. Still a girl. Still a girl. It was a kind, well-meaning chorus, but it only underscored the difference. A girl who never had to question her place as a girl rarely needed to be told she was *still a girl*.

"But I can see it on your face sometimes," her grandmother said. "You still question it. And there's so much fuss about Alarie girls."

"That you thought it would prove something about me." Isla didn't mean to put such a chill into her own voice.

"Prove something to yourself, mija," her grandmother said. "You have nothing to prove to anyone else."

It was a lovely sentiment.

And it was as fictional as a fairy tale. It was no more true than the folklore other children evoked when Isla was in school, saying Isla could curse cows, or that stolen blood ran through her veins.

"If you wanted it for me, then why did you send Renata?" Isla asked.

"This was for the both of you," Abuela said. "To give you standing no one could question. Renata loved that part most of all. Much as we both adore your sister, we can't pretend she doesn't have a petty streak. She was absolutely entranced by the thought of the two of you holding the Alarie status over any snob who crosses your path."

Before they had left, Renata had treated the Alarie House like a novelty, a glamorous adventure that would give them a thousand stories to tell. But Renata had not only wanted what they might find at the Alarie House.

She had thought Isla needed it.

FIVE

AS ISLA LAY IN her bed, she tried to keep it close, the anger she'd felt toward her sister the last time they'd spoken. She wanted to polish it to a shine like one of those pretty jewels in the Alarie House walls. If it stayed bright and brilliant enough, it might hold off the guilt pressing in like the chill off the window glass.

But without Renata, their room felt lopsided. Without Renata, the whole world felt a little lopsided.

Renata had been the reason this room was as raucously gorgeous as it was. When they had chosen the drapes, the current style had been for girls to adorn their rooms in shades of rose, cream, and lemon so subtle you could barely tell them apart. But Renata had danced around the room, taking Isla's hands and declaring, "Let's do something that thrills us!"

And so the room had ended up in Renata's favorite reds and violets, and the greens and blues that reminded Isla of her favorite books in Abuela's library. The brocades and damasks were as luxurious as they were old-fashioned, all fabrics that could have been right out of Renata's most cherished romantic novels. The gold cords on the curtains were considered gaudy and tacky, and they adored them all the more for it.

Isla reached for the letters that had been sitting, unopened.

Dear Isla,

Do you remember the night of Caroline Beegan's engagement party? I was thinking of it as Luisa was quizzing us on how to word invitations so that guests will know what to wear.

You know me well. You always have. So you knew from the day we received Caroline's invitation that I had been plotting my revenge. Really, I had been plotting my revenge from the day she called Abuela a husbandless old hag.

When I told you I wanted to get back at our dear Caroline, I feared you might ask, "What for?" But you remembered. You too had been storing up that particular insult with as much fervor as I had.

Our necklaces that night were works of art, weren't they? I felt like a swan wearing all those pink diamonds. And in that strand of yellow diamonds, you looked like an autumn sun. I can still remember the face of the bride-to-be, how she was just soaked in envy. Not only for the jewels themselves, but how everyone's eyes followed them.

And we timed it perfectly, didn't we? Just as the speeches were beginning, we each broke a diamond out of its setting and popped it into our mouths. Do you remember how the cracking sound made the room fall silent? Do you remember how all eyes found us?

I do. And I remember being a little surprised at just how much of the room turned their attention to us.

You, mi hermanita, weren't fazed in the least. You just cracked another diamond out of your necklace and ate it.

We were magnificent, you and I. We stared back at everyone, wondering how long it would take them to realize that our priceless diamonds were candy. If memory serves, the old ladies with their evening tea caught the joke first. I can still hear them stifling laughs as long as they could and then cackling when they couldn't. (Did I ever tell you that they all asked Abuela if she'd put us up to it?)

I must tell you that in retrospect, I do feel a little bad for the bride-to-be, flying from the room, inconsolable. Well, at least until she was plied with more champagne and a few of her engagement gifts.

Even now, sugar dissolving on my tongue reminds me of that party.

We were infamous that night, you and me, the girls who ate the jewels right out of their own necklaces.

I miss you, Isla. But I also know that you don't forgive easily. Neither do I. If I did, I never would have gone to such lengths to teach our darling Miss Beegan a lesson. And if you did, you never would have been my partner in revenge. So how can I hold it against you if you hold my own words against me?

R.

Isla remembered everything from that night. And Renata knew that. Yet that spectacular little viper had written to Isla as though perhaps it had all slipped Isla's mind.

Renata knew that every little recollection would reach its fingers into Isla's chest, getting a solid grasp on her heart.

And it worked. Isla hated that it worked, but it did.

Isla opened the last letter.

Dear Isla,

Since you haven't answered—and I know from Abuela that you've gotten my letters—I won't bother you with any more. But I do hope that when I return home you'll talk to me. I'm your sister. Do you really think you can be rid of me this easily?

R.

An ember still flared in the center of Isla. But it had cooled from anger to annoyance. And Renata had lit something else alongside it.

It was enough to send Isla downstairs. It was enough to make her light the stove, the blue of the flames illuminating the dim kitchen. Isla melted sugar alcohol until it looked like blown glass. Heat breathed off the bubbling surface. She stirred in dye, and poured it all into the same molds she and Renata had used the night before that engagement party.

Renata was right. They were never rid of each other, easily or otherwise. They were a wonderfully, wickedly matched set. Instead of proper shoes, they wore dirty ballet slippers under their dresses, their skirts long enough to hide the gray-ing canvas unless they were running across a lawn. They wore eyebrow-raising color combinations too garish for polite company—bright yellow and sea blue, purple and straw-berry red—with dyed enaguas underneath so that a third and fourth color flashed as they walked. When Renata received a proposal from a young man later heard to say that women were better as ornaments—"pretty, silent, ideally moving only enough to flatter the light"—she kept the ring. She never went anywhere without it, as though perpetually making a point. She and Isla used the diamond to scratch secret mes-sages onto the windows of those they admired and those they loathed.

Isla settled the molds. The juice and pulp from the pitaya had turned the sugar alcohol a bright, deep pink. It was the shade of the rarest pink sapphires, jewels worthy of welcom-ing home the infamous Renata Soler.

SIX

WHEN THE CANDY GEMS had hardened and cooled, Isla placed them in the settings of the same necklaces she and Renata had worn to the engagement party. She left the better of the two on Renata's dresser, in a velvet box, lid open. If it was worth doing, Renata had taught her, it was worth doing to excess.

Except that the girl who returned home later that week was as far from Renata Soler as those jewels were from true gemstones.

"I so wish you'd stayed and seen more of the house." Renata's voice was high and tinkling as bells on a Christmas wreath. "You think you saw jewels everywhere? You didn't see the half of them. Set into the corners, the railings, even the desks in the lesson room. You can't even count them. Rumor has it they're gifts from families overcome with gratitude for what their daughters have learned, but las Señoras are far too modest to confirm it."

Was there a punch line here? Had Renata stolen a few right out of the walls as she said her farewells?

If someone had turned Renata into a doll version of herself, that would be the girl sitting at the dining room table now. She reached for the salt shaker as though blessing it. The curls that usually bounced around her face as she talked had been pinned out of her eyes. Even if they hadn't been, her upper body was so still they might not have moved anyway. Her shoulders seemed to occupy the same point in space for the entire meal. *This* was the sister who used to gesture so much when she talked that she knocked over glasses and tureens?

Abuela looked as though the soup disagreed with her. With one glance toward Isla, she spoke without a word. That look of indigestion said, *I wanted her polished, not pretentious.*

"And the girls are just the most excellent company." Renata cut her food into pieces so small that Isla nearly checked whether she was feeding a miniature dog under the table. Where was the Renata who ate tacos dorados de papa with a passion that no romantic hero could match, her fingers glossed in oil and hierbas?

Not a crumb landed on the table or on her. Her white dress—which Alarie sister had sent her home in this? Renata never passed up a chance to wear color—turned faintly golden from the candles on the table. Isla and Abuela had both put on dark gowns in celebration of Renata's first dinner home, and now their dresses flanked hers like fine, heavy drapes around pale, sunlit sheers.

Renata took a delicate sip from her glass of vino tinto. "The ones with whom I just commenced, they're going to be lifelong friends, I can already tell."

Commenced? Was this the finishing school translation of graduated?

"One has already invited us all out to her country house," Renata said.

Her *country* house? Renata said it so casually. As though it was the most natural thing in the world to have enough houses that one needed to specify.

Isla kept waiting for Renata to cast off this version of herself like an overly fussy coat. What need did she have to put on perfect manners in front of them? Isla was her sister, and Abuela had always done whatever she wanted despite any hint of scandal. She had traveled alone since she was Renata's age. She had worn whatever length gloves she preferred in a time when they were as carefully calibrated as watches. For whom exactly was Renata performing?

Abuela slipped Isla another meaningful look between bites of enmoladas. It was a flash of resignation tinged with the slightest eye roll, as though to say, *This was my idea. I suppose it serves me right.*

"And they weren't nearly as proud as you'd think." Renata

said this directly to Isla before turning to Abuela. "When I told them we do all our own cooking ourselves, they sounded envious. 'Oh, I wish I knew how to do anything in the kitchen. It's the room I'm most useless in.' I felt very sorry for them."

"Yes." Abuela sipped her wine. "The heart does bleed for those who've never washed a dish, doesn't it?"

Poor Abuela was regretting every string she'd pulled to send them to the Alarie House. One granddaughter had come back fast as a returning train. The other came back as an imitation of herself. She was like a character in a ballet, reduced to basic features and symbolic moments, a girl written for the stage instead of real life.

Guilt pinched harder at Isla. Maybe she should have told Abuela more about what had happened. Maybe Isla shouldn't have left Renata around the other Alarie girls. But Isla had never imagined that they would rub off on her this much, that she would imitate them so completely.

Isla had been sure Renata would be the one to rub off on them. Where were the tales of her convincing other girls to wear garish lingerie under their dresses, an invisible joke on their instructors? Where were the stories of Renata spinning through that prim house, dethroning queens and summoning chaos?

Renata didn't even give up the act when she and Isla were alone in their room. She greeted the candy jewels with excitement that seemed choreographed. "Oh," she said, in a voice as delicate as Abuela's mantillas. "Isn't this lovely?"

She held up the necklace. The candy jewels looked pink or red depending on how they took the light. There was almost a wink of the old Renata mischief as she looked through them and said, "You shouldn't have."

It was enough to buoy Isla into holding up her own identical strand. "Oh, but I had to."

Then, just as quickly, that wink was gone. Renata put down the candy jewels. She started brushing her hair and turned back to the featherlight chatter of, "It's just the loveliest place. I do wish you'd stayed. You would have fallen in love as much as I did."

"What are you doing?" Isla asked.

Renata paused the brush halfway down her hair. "I'm getting ready for bed." She met Isla's eyes in the mirror of her dressing table. "Beauty sleep may not be exciting"—her words were almost a trill, a chirp—"but neither of us is getting any younger, are we?"

Isla was seventeen. Renata would be twenty in November.

"No, I mean, what are you doing?" Isla gestured at the whole of her sister.

Her perpetually windblown hair was fastened in ways that made her look like a society wife, rather than a girl who would climb on a roof to listen in on a conversation. The film of her white nightgown trailed behind her. It looked ghostly against their bedroom, like a spiderweb on Abuela's hydrangeas.

The act Renata was putting on would have been laugh-able if it hadn't been such an eerily accurate impression of the other girls at the Alarie House.

"This isn't you," Isla said. "You're not you."

Renata shrugged a shoulder, and the film of her night-gown sleeve fluttered. "And you're not what you could have been if you'd stayed long enough to learn something."

The words landed and stung. Then the sting of them twisted into anger.

Staring right at Renata in the mirror, Isla pressed her thumb against a candy jewel in her own necklace. She pushed into the center of the jewel until it gave and popped out. It left a hollow where it had been, the metal setting an empty frame. Isla put the gem in her mouth, the slightly off sweetness of the artificial sugar brightened by pitaya. She let the red flash on her tongue.

Some might have called it immature. Isla preferred to think of it as petty. And the sister Isla knew considered pet-tiness an art form. She had taught it to Isla the same way she'd taught her to sneak sips of champagne, to go barefoot through statue gardens and then get her shoes on before any-one saw, how to steal profiteroles from just the right spot on the croquembouche that no one would notice.

As for the sister in front of her now, Isla didn't recognize her. The sister in front of her now had forgotten her own sharp, glittering heart, and it just made Isla want to scan-dalize her more. It made Isla hold the candy jewel between her teeth like a garnet made of blood. For all Isla cared, this Renata could throw off the candy jewels and switch them out for pearls to clutch.

But Renata's hands did not throw aside the candy jewels. Or push away the velvet box. They didn't reach for a proper strand of pearls. Nor did they continue to work the brush down her hair.

Instead, Renata's hands reached for the letter opener on their shared desk.

She turned around, wielding it like a dagger.

SEVEN

RENATA PLUNGED THE LETTER opener through the air.

Isla held the necklace out between them. She pulled each end tight in one hand, stretching it taut.

The letter opener stabbed into another candy jewel. It exploded into pink shards.

Isla twisted the necklace and wrenched the letter opener away, the scrolling loops of the handle caught in the delicate chain.

Her sister reeled back, eyes wide.

In that stare, Isla saw the whirl of everything at once. Renata looked terrified of both Isla and herself. Then her expression flashed to the vacant gaze of those girls at the

Alarie House. Then there was a lightning bolt of something else. Rage.

But as fast as it appeared, it vanished, like Renata had torn it out of herself.

Renata had so much anger toward Isla. Yet she couldn't express it. She had sealed it under the veneer of finishing school charm. And when she couldn't keep it there, it broke through, sudden and violent and shocking them both.

Two fears chased Isla from the room, like twinned shadows. They were hard and chilled and a perfectly matched set. Fear of her sister. Fear for her sister.

Isla ran down the hall, her dark nightgown flying behind her. All around her loomed the tall, stately portraits of ancestors that Abuela had commissioned herself, to give the impression that they had been in the family for generations, that their family had, of course, always had their portraits painted.

Growing up, Isla and Renata had talked to these gowned and suited figures as though they were living relatives who might dispense advice or tell thrilling tales.

Now those faces twisted in judgment. They were nightmare versions of themselves, growing taller and more scornful with each step Isla took.

The whole way down the hall, Isla called out to Abuela. She was so loud that Abuela was already out of her bed, on her feet, and at her door by the time Isla reached out to knock.

"What is it?" Abuela blinked into the hallway light. Without her lipstick and her eyebrow pencil, she looked like a tracing paper version of herself. "What's happened?"

The words for any explanation jumbled in Isla's mouth. They dissolved on her tongue. All she could get out was "It's Renata."

EIGHT

BUT RENATA WASN'T IN their room anymore.

She wasn't as she had been so many times, reading her favorite novels in bed, a whole stack of them piled up on the covers as though she never knew which one she might want until she climbed into the sheets.

She wasn't down the hall, opening the linen cupboard with a wicked smile, rearranging the perfect order of Abuela's cloths and pillowcases.

She wasn't at the bathroom sink, combing her dark curls until they shone like twists of black silk.

There was no sign Renata had been in the room except the whisper of billowing white at the window. Night air filled the delicate sails of the sheer curtain linings.

Isla drew toward them slowly, as hopeful as she was apprehensive. This was one of her sister's jokes. It had to be. Once she came close enough, once she looked well and truly worried, Renata would leap from behind the curtains, laughing furiously. She would immediately soften the sting of the joke by making Isla part of it. *We've got to try that sometime! The both of us, one on each side! We could get Imogene back for last Halloween!*

But when the sheers drifted aside, they revealed nothing but a square of dark sky and the silhouettes of distant trees. There was nothing here but the glint off the pink shards on the floor, and the open window, the same window Isla and Renata had snuck out of together so many times.

NINE

ISLA FLEW DOWNSTAIRS. SHE threw the door open and ran out of the house. She didn't even close it behind her, so her own name echoed through the air in her grandmother's voice.

Isla ran past Abuela's hydrangeas, looking for Renata against the globes of pink and blue flowers. She dashed toward the live oaks at the back of the house, where branches screened the garden from the road.

But Renata wasn't under their boughs. She wasn't where their shadows interlaced like fingers.

The grass was damp under Isla's feet, the hem of her nightgown heavier as it settled. Her breathing stung in her chest.

Renata had gone so gracefully, so quickly, that there was no sign of her. Nothing in the dark told her secrets. Even the ground, the trees, the night gave no hint of which way she'd gone.

When Isla looked back toward their window, a small star winked from inside the room.

Isla followed it back upstairs.

Renata had left her ring on her dresser, the diamond she'd used to scratch messages on window glass, the one she never went anywhere without. That had to mean she was coming back.

But in the morning, she was still lost to them.

TEN

IF THE SOLER GIRLS had turned out as gauche and shameless as wearing a white dress in a rainstorm, everyone blamed their grandmother. Abuela did what she pleased, too busy with her business contracts and her gardening to care what anyone thought. She knelt in the dirt and then greeted visitors in her gardening shoes. She refinished cast-off furniture herself instead of buying it new, to hell with anyone who came in the door and spotted their old credenza. She chose the paint color of this house because she liked it. Neighbors considered it too green, aggressively green, they said, but Abuela seemed to drift past such comments with willful and blissful ignorance. In her full skirts, she'd climbed up on the roof after storms to check the caps on the chimneys, and when she was too old to do it, she'd taught Isla and Renata to, in full view of the scandalized neighbors.

And she'd raised two girls as though it was no more trouble than having a couple of house cats. Abuela did what she set her mind to. So when she told Isla, "We'll find her," Isla knew she meant it.

Doubt still slipped off Isla's tongue. "How?"

"Every friend and acquaintance I have is watching for her," Abuela said.

Translation: We're going to have to find her ourselves.

The authorities had spoken their piece late last night. Renata was an adult. She could vanish if she liked. And though they hadn't said it, Isla could read their faces. They considered her disappearance the act of a flighty, impetuous girl.

Isla had left the candy jewels where they were, next to Renata's bed. As though something so pathetically small was going to be the thing to call her home.

The kettle whistled, and Isla got up to pour the water.

They had been sitting at the kitchen table. Some things were too bleak and too real for the dining room. They both wore sweaters over their nightgowns. It was the first time Isla could remember seeing her grandmother this way. Isla and Renata, yes, often. Abuela called them *las haraganas* when they lazed around on holiday mornings, hair unbrushed. Not Abuela. Even when she'd had fevers, she rose and dressed unless she was too shaky to get out of bed, and even then, she drew on her eyebrows and put on her lipstick while lying down, a hand mirror propped up on pillows.

Guilt got its teeth deeper into Isla.

"This is my fault," she said as she sank back down into a chair. It felt less like a confession than voicing something that had been hanging in the air.

"No, it isn't." Abuela set her wrinkled hand on Isla's. "And there's no use wearing yourself out thinking otherwise."

It was as startling as it was comforting. Her grandmother had always managed to be encouraging without being particularly affectionate. When she and Renata brought home good results on exams, they were met not with joyful hugs but with, *Well, we must do something to celebrate, mustn't we?* When Isla had had the trouble with the other girls at school, there hadn't been any, *oh, mija.* There had been Abuela making a list of the girls' parents and saying, *Good. A swift guide to those I never need bother doing business with again. I do enjoy streamlining.*

It made physical consolation a little alarming. Abuela only gave it when things were truly dire.

"I left her there," Isla said.

"And she chose to stay there." Her grandmother's palm was soft, a little cold from poor circulation. "Just as she chose to leave here tonight. Her choices are her own."

Were they? Renata had probably felt obligated to go to the Alarie House so Isla didn't have to go alone, and she'd chosen to make the best of it, to get what she could out of it.

And then Isla had run. Isla had left her.

Isla had disappointed Abuela. But she had abandoned Renata. And in abandoning her, she'd lost her.

She'd started losing her that first night at the Alarie House. From that first night, Isla should have known better than to leave Renata alone.

ELEVEN

NO PART OF THE Alarie House was engraved more deeply into Isla's mind than the foyer.

Every hallway met in that center room. Above it, a chandelier hung from the high ceiling, glittering with every color jewel Isla had ever seen or heard of.

Below, the floor was a perfect square. On each side, it dropped down two steps to a sunken atrium. Each step was tall enough that they could have been used as benches, if Alarie girls ever were to do something so indecorous as gathering on the floor.

That sunken atrium had been paved with renderings of princess-cut jewels on white tile. Each painted jewel was a different color, as though reflecting the gems in the chandelier above. Even the grout between the tiles shimmered, as though the floor had been mortared with gold.

Isla's dreams that first night had sparkled, but not in the way of lovely things. They sparkled like the glare of harsh daylight off water.

She'd never been a sleepwalker, and yet she'd woken up kneeling on that tile. She didn't remember coming down the stairs, or down those steps.

She registered the chill of metal in her palms. She was holding a heavy hand mirror, pewter hilt down. In her sleep, she'd heard hammering she couldn't locate, and now, in the horror of waking up, she knew what it was.

A crack snaked through two of the painted princess-cut jewels, one red, one green.

Isla had just damaged the Alarie House.

The Alarie sisters had the favor of a hundred powerful families, on multiple continents. Abuela had said it herself. Whatever they thought of a girl, whatever they thought of her family, became as good as the truth. And Isla had already made a wreck of everything. This wasn't Renata's shameless, insouciant charm. This made Isla look mad, destructive, and it would make all of them look mad and destructive.

White apparitions drifted near the ceiling.

A dozen Alarie girls were above her. They stood on the mezzanine that framed the high chandelier and overlooked the foyer. They rested their hands on the wrought iron railings as lightly as ballerinas. Their faces and arms ran from pale to dark. Their heights ranged from shorter than Isla to even taller than Abuela. Some of their bodies were thin as the wispy silver of their necklaces, some full and soft as Renata's favorite actress.

Yet they all looked alike. Their unrevealing expressions and their white nightgowns made them girls in a dance corps, a flock of swans in a ballet.

Their stares converged on her as though she was the lowest point of a cut diamond.

She didn't belong here. Those girls knew it. They had the fixed gazes of knowing things they should have no way of knowing. They had known what she would do before she'd done it, and they'd gathered to watch. They could see inside her, and they looked at her as though they were perfect diamonds and she was quartz with a glaring occlusion at the center. Her cells were flaws. Her heart was an impurity in the shell of her body. They could see inside her, and they wanted her gone. They wanted to keep the better Soler sister and eject the lesser one.

At least that was what Isla had thought until last night.

This was supposed to be so good for you, Abuela had said.

It could have been good for both of them if Isla hadn't left Renata. There was something precious they could earn at the Alarie House, an imprint of approval. But they could only get it while living among those strange, staring girls. And because Isla had left Renata alone with them, their madness had swallowed Renata.

The only way Isla could find her again was inside it.

"I have to go back," Isla said.

Abuela took a slow, steadying breath. "If she'd gone back there, we would have heard from the Alaries. You're no more likely to find her there than here."

"And when we do find her?" Isla asked. "Then what? We all politely discuss flower arranging? You saw how she was. She could still be gone from us even if she's in the same house."

A constellation of things converged at once to make Abuela look younger. The uncertainty pinching her face into an unfamiliar expression. The flush in her cheeks from late-night visits to neighbors, hurried phone call after hurried phone call. The pieces of her hair falling down from the way she'd arranged it, with so much more haste than usual. Her typical peinado could withstand a September windstorm and still maintain its orderly coil.

"I let you both down," Isla said.

"No, you didn't," her grandmother said.

"I let her down. And I think she hates me for it."

"You sister could never hate you."

"I wouldn't blame her," Isla said.

If Isla had stayed with Renata, the haunting blankness of those girls never would have touched her. Isla and Renata would have been the same Soler girls they'd always been, smiling sweetly whenever they needed to, raising hell whenever they could. That had been Renata's plan from the start, for them to learn just enough of the choreography to pass as finishing school girls. And Isla had been too much of a coward to stick to it.

"I left her," Isla said.

Abuela looked as though she wanted to strike a pen through this conversation, like a clause in a contract she didn't much care for.

"If we don't know what happened to her, we can't really know her," Isla said. "So even if we find her, if we don't know how to reach her, we could lose her again."

"You're her sister," Abuela said. "You will always be able to reach her."

"Except that I couldn't," Isla said. "And if I don't understand where she's been, what she's been through, who she is now, who she's become, maybe I never will."

Isla knew now what Renata had been trying to tell her. If Isla didn't face the Alarie girls, she'd be afraid forever. She'd be the little girl scared of the other girls at school. She'd be the sleepwalker skittering away from the stares of finishing school students. She had to go back to the Alarie House, for Renata, and to know she could.

Renata was an Alarie girl, and Isla wasn't, and as long as that was true, they were on two different sides of a door, lost to each other.

"You're going to find her." Isla held out her hand as though this were one of Abuela's business deals. "And I'm going to find out how we really get her back."

Slowly, Abuela took Isla's hand. "I know you. And you're

as bad as she is. If I forbid you, you'll be out that window next."

Isla gave the kind of firm, authoritative handshake Abuela had taught her. Confident. Fearless. Matching that of any man. It was an exact copy of the one Abuela gave every time, to every new acquaintance, to every business associate, even as age stiffened her fingers.

"I'm doing this right this time," Isla said. "For her and for me."

If Isla had to go through those lovely, unnerving girls to find Renata again, to find what Abuela had wanted for both of them, she would do it.

As Isla packed, Renata's diamond ring sparkled from her dresser. The edges were jagged, sharp enough to slash, the reason Renata had loved it in the first place.

Isla slipped it onto her own finger. She would wear it to finishing school, a glittering claw on her hand.

This time, she wouldn't run.

TWELVE

ISLA RETURNED TO THAT house of crisp white walls and wrought iron trim, those rooms of tiled and planked floors, graceful arches, tall wooden doors. She returned to the school where it was the most ordinary thing in the world to see polished gems set into the walls. Even the staircase had been inlaid with square-cut stones at the same intervals as the balusters.

Somewhere on the second floor, in those branching hallways, was a vacant room Isla could talk her way into.

She just needed to convince the exquisite woman before whom she now sat.

"I am truly sorry," Isla said, "for my inexcusable behavior."

Luisa Alarie's face, sculpted meticulously as an artist's frieze, gave away nothing.

The Alarie sisters' office wasn't a gray room of file cabinets and undusted shelves. It was as opulent as the rest of the house, with gems placed into the walls. There were even jewels set into the raw wood beams crossing the low ceiling. The colors seemed to have been scattered at random, but the chaos was precisely curated, all colors in conversation with those around them.

"When I think of it," Isla said, "I barely recognize myself."

The best lies, Renata had taught her, were woven like fine cloth. Use truth as the warp, weave in anything invented as if it were the weft.

"I'm speechless just thinking of how I conducted myself," Isla said.

Abuela had done her best by letter and telephone call. *The rest*—she had told Isla—*is up to you.*

"It was quite puzzling to us all that you left so suddenly," Luisa said. "Nearly as puzzling as you returning to us now."

Luisa looked as though she was perpetually appraising anyone before her. Her features were severe, her nose sharp enough to cut a tea cake, the features of a woman who might have modeled for a department store.

The first time Isla had seen the Alarie sisters, they had looked as distinct from each other as the signature colors they wore. Alba was very short, but something about her carriage and the sheer length of her eyelashes made her look tall if you weren't standing right next to her. Eduarda had large, almost mischievous eyes, and her hair was fine and straight, two tidy curtains on either side of her face. But different as they looked, they were each the kind of strikingly beautiful you would never call pretty. *Pretty* would have been too soft a word. *Pretty* did not encompass the trembling awe these women inspired. They had been born lovely, and then sculpted each gesture and glance into pin-sharp perfection.

"We must, of course," Luisa said, "address the obvious question."

Tiny points of heat beaded on the back of Isla's neck.

Here it came, the calling to account, the settling of debts. Isla had damaged Alarie House property. Of course the bill would come due.

"When a girl leaves in the middle of the night, she gives a clear message of how little she wishes to be somewhere," Luisa said. "So when your grandmother called to ask if you might return, I could only assume she was insisting you do so."

Isla pressed her hands onto the edges of the chair seat, trying to make her relief less obvious. No mention of the damaged floor. Only offense at Isla running out without a word.

"We do prefer to take on girls who are truly dedicated to this process," Luisa said. "And you might forgive me questioning your dedication."

Isla wove in a little more truth to sell the lie.

"I wasn't sure I'd find my place among the other girls," she said. "But since leaving, I've realized that an accomplished young lady doesn't turn away from a challenge."

The lie landed. Isla could almost hear it finding its mark, like the fletching of an arrow vibrating. Luisa Alarie's face changed. It was no longer reserved and evaluating. The slight lift to Luisa Alarie's chin no longer seemed meant to remind Isla that she was a supplicant. Now it seemed almost optimistic, an expression of, *There might be hope for you yet.*

"If your sister is any indication"—Luisa Alarie rose from her chair, upholstered in the most elegant black brocade Isla had ever seen, and Isla rose in response—"you have a bright future ahead of you here."

Luisa Alarie looked so proudly encouraging that she clearly didn't know Renata had run off. Isla certainly wasn't about to tell her.

"I should mention"—Luisa paused—"enough time has passed since you were first enrolled that all the girls who were here then have graduated. You'll have to become acquainted with everyone all over again."

As though Isla had made such good friends the first time.

"The silver lining, of course, is that no one was there to witness your surprising departure," Luisa said. "You'll have a fresh beginning. And I do think that the surest way to move on from something is not to dwell on it. Best to put all this behind us, don't you agree?"

The bargain was clear. Don't cause a scene, and neither will anyone else. They knew what Isla had done to the floor; of course they knew. The crack in the tile had surely already been repaired, and they would all pretend it had never existed in the first place. It was now up to Isla to prove she was not the girl she'd been that night.

"Of course," Isla said.

"Welcome to the Alarie House." Luisa offered Isla her hand, and Isla took it.

As soon as Isla shook, Luisa drew her hand back as though Isla's palm was hot glass. "Oh, goodness," she said. "We'll have to work on that, won't we? We can't have you shaking hands like a horse groom."

That was the one thing Isla thought she already knew how to do. Was Isla supposed to tilt her wrist down like a young lady from the last century offering her hand to be kissed? Was she supposed to let her fingers flop like wilting stems? *An uncertain handshake only shows your adversary that you will be uncertain in your dealings,* Abuela had taught her.

"Don't worry." Luisa's dress was blue fog around the edge of her desk. "The most promising girls we meet are so often the ones with the most room to improve."

THIRTEEN

THE SUREST WAY TO *move on from something,* Luisa Alarie had said, *is not to dwell on it.*

But Isla couldn't take her eyes off the foyer floor.

The crack was still there, running through the fine tile work. Maybe they wanted it there to remind her. Or they wanted her to prove she could walk past something unpleasant and ignore it. But as Isla carried her bags through the foyer, her gaze kept crawling toward the sunken atrium.

She tried to look at anything else. Above her was that tiered chandelier, so sprawling and magnificent she couldn't imagine the cables necessary to hold it up. Real jewels had to be heavier than leaded glass. Garnets and sapphires cast down candied light. Finials hanging from the point of the basket shone green or peach pink like peridot and morganite.

The interior of the foyer winked back the sun that came through the windows. Long, decorative mirrors doubled and tripled the gems' glitter. Strands of gold veined the wallpaper and wood, each precious stone held in a pronged setting worthy of a fine necklace.

Supposedly, the stones were gifts from grateful families, delighted by how their daughters had turned out. More salacious rumors, whispered with teacups shielding the lips, spoke of families attempting to bribe the Alarie sisters to gain their daughters' admission.

As Isla passed a mirror, a shimmering blur dashed by, like a ghost wearing a pale sequin gown. Her brain told her it was the cut stones throwing their light around. But her brain wasn't fast enough to stop her body from startling and turning.

And slamming right into someone she hadn't known was there.

"Easy." The girl put her hands on Isla's upper arms, not as though she was holding her away. More like she was keeping her in place. "I don't recommend sudden movements around here." She dropped her voice to a whisper. "Too many sharp edges."

Her dark hair was fastened low at the nape of her neck with a silver clip. Her trouser suit was as immaculately pressed and free of lint as Abuela's dresses. It was cut in a more feminine way than Isla had ever seen, drawn in at the waist almost like a toreador's cummerbund. It was the kind of ensemble that girls usually only wore in the city. Yet here this one was, far enough from the nearest town that few roads were paved.

"Paz Nieves," the girl said, offering her hand. Her stance emphasized the curves under her tailored shirt. She wasn't trying to downplay them. She wasn't trying to downplay anything.

Isla took Paz's hand, and before she could remember her first lesson from Luisa Alarie, she shook it just as Abuela had taught her. Too firmly.

Paz's hand more than matched it, the gesture small, firm, and decisive. "So she has conviction."

"Accosting our newest student before she's even reached her room?" Eduarda Alarie appeared like a whirl of lemon cream, her dress layered in pale yellow. She wore her usual necklace of sizable but tasteful yellow stones, bright and glossed-looking as candied lemon slices topping a pie. Her skin looked like a paler version of her light brown hair, the same color but thinned out, like a tint of a paint. Her eyes were deep amber, and they shimmered with the scanning movements of someone who could monitor thirty-five girls at the same time. She had the slow, easy grace of a woman Abuela's age, but when Isla had first met Eduarda, she'd been surprised to see she looked only a few years older than Renata.

"Not accosting," Paz said. "Greeting. Welcoming."

"You've been given a second chance, young lady," Eduarda Alarie said. "Don't waste it. And don't let this one scare you." She glanced toward Paz and then back at Isla.

"Have I been anything but a perfect gentleman?" Paz lifted Isla's suitcases. "I'm even helping her to her room."

"Paz has been kind enough to play the gentlemen in many of our lessons lately. Hence her"—Eduarda seemed to be searching for a tactful word—"flamboyant attire."

"She's trying to explain me," Paz whispered.

Eduarda waved a hand in the same manner she might dismiss a little brother she found irritating. Then she was off down a hallway.

As though calculating when Eduarda would be out of earshot, Paz seemed to count a precise number of seconds in her head. Then she asked, "Will you be needing a fainting couch yet?"

"Excuse me?" Isla asked.

"Have I shocked you?" Paz asked. "With my flamboyant attire?"

This girl had no idea what it would take to shock her.

"No," Isla said.

"She's fine," Paz called down the hallway.

"I am so very glad to hear it, Paz"—Eduarda projected her voice without even seeming to raise it—"but what have we said about yelling?"

Paz kept her eyes on Isla. "Welcome to the Alarie House. Where your interest in anything beyond table arrangements goes to die."

Her voice was rich and textured, with a deep, melodic

tone that seemed part innate, part finishing school. But her words were pinched with warning. *Leave now while you still can.*

No chance. Isla wasn't leaving this time. Everything she needed to know was in this house.

FOURTEEN

GIRLS MILLED INTO THE dining room, each looking ready for a summer picnic. They all had gently arranged hair and wore dresses in blues, greens, and pinks as faint and subtle as milk glass.

They laughed in clusters as they made their way to the impossibly long dining table. Their postures were as upright and rigid as the stems of wineglasses. When they crossed the windows, filled with thickening evening light, they became elegant silhouettes.

The dining room table was a field of spotless glasses and polished flatware, and the sun turned the sterling silver to copper and the crystal to fire.

"Good evening, ladies," Luisa Alarie said, her sisters following a half step behind.

At the sound of Luisa's voice, every girl took her place just behind a chair.

On Abuela's recommendation, Isla was dressed just like them. She wore a dress as filmy as poured milk and as pale as almond cream. But she didn't move with them the way they so automatically seemed to move with each other. They were a Degas painting, just with longer skirts.

The sun glinted off Eduarda's neck, transforming the stones to a seam of gold like the horizon line. Luisa and Alba wore almost identically cut necklaces, but in different colors. Luisa's heavy blue stones—topaz maybe—matched her gown, deeper than the dress she'd had on earlier.

Alba Alarie wore a gown like lavender smoke. At her throat was a heavy amethyst necklace that filled with light as the Alarie sisters spaced themselves out, Luisa at one end, second-eldest Alba at the other, youngest Eduarda in the middle.

The girls sat down in perfect synchronization, a beat after the Alarie sisters seated themselves. Isla tried to time herself alongside them. She placed her napkin on her lap in the same moment they did. The napkins were heavy and bleached white, but they were also satin slick. As the girls placed them, it looked as though they were unfurling dozens of white lilies.

They all passed cassoulets and platters of vegetables, following the same precise instincts for when to let the weight of a dish go, when to help your dining companion serve herself. Isla remembered this part, the courtesy and attention it took to keep it all from spilling while not holding anything at an awkward angle. *If you can keep your dresses pristine handing sauces to each other*, Alba had told them the last time Isla was here, *you'll be more than ready for a fine restaurant or a dinner party.*

From Isla's right, a flicker of honeysuckle perfume lapped through the smells of herbs and roux. The girl sitting next to Isla was pretty, small, her body soft and rounded. And she had a knife-glint of mischief in her face that reminded Isla of her sister.

The pink of her dress and the brown of her skin both warmed and brightened each other. The fabric was a dusky shade of rose, but against the watercolor-light fabrics around the table, it seemed vivid as the magenta bougainvillea dripping off the roof.

"I'm Carina." The words bubbled out of the girl's mouth like a laugh. "I saw your name on the chores ledger. We're weeding the side flower beds together after dinner." She was frothy as champagne punch, and her undiluted effervescence made any resemblance to Renata vanish. "I think I'm a door or two down from you. My room's the messiest, that's how you can tell. Borrow anything you want."

Unlikely. Even sitting down, Isla could tell Carina had to be half a head shorter than her. Carina had fuller breasts, a smaller waist, and comically smaller feet. Cinderella small. Isla's hips *might* have fit into one of Carina's belled skirts, but that would have been it. Isla had a broad rib cage that always surprised dressmakers—*How were you hiding that? It's like an aviary under there*—and she didn't fill out the chest of anything without stuffing her brassiere.

As Eduarda said an angelic prayer to bless the food, Isla's napkin began to slide. Silky as a pocket square, it slipped away like liquid.

She grabbed it just before it wafted to the floor.

At the sudden movement, Carina opened one eye, and then shut it.

As Eduarda asked the Lord's blessing on the lovely girls they'd just sent out into the world and the ones they'd recently welcomed, Isla pressed the napkin against her thighs.

Again, it slid.

Carina was the only other girl not perfectly still, eyes closed, during the prayer. She shifted in her seat as though trying to get comfortable.

Isla was attempting to pinch the napkin between her knees when she caught a flash of pale pink and silver.

Just under the table, Carina was holding a safety pin between her varnished nails.

Isla looked at her sideways.

Carina showed Isla her own napkin. A dash of silver ticked through the cloth. She had pinned the napkin to the waist of her dress.

Isla took the pin and did the same with her own napkin.

It stayed, floating on her lap.

It was such small magic, and yet it was as though a trapdoor had opened in her brain. Until this moment, Isla had never considered that such sterling femininity might be made of a series of certain tricks, and that it was matter of learning enough of them. "You're welcome," Carina whispered, dipping her head in saintly reverence just in time for the *Amen*.

Maybe Isla had been right about the Alarie girls, that they just knew things. But maybe she had also been wrong about them. Maybe they had been staring at her not because of what they could tell just by looking at her. Maybe they had been waiting for Isla to understand what they already understood, to learn what they already knew.

FIFTEEN

"**E** **DUARDA SAYS IT'S ALWAYS** worse after windy days." Carina tied the lavender ribbon of a gardening hat under her chin. "All kinds of seeds blow. You have to keep an eye on everything. And this time of year, you've got to do it this late. You have to give the bees their space."

The Alarie House was a sealed system. Isla had learned that her first time here. There was no one working here apart from the Alarie sisters themselves, who did most of the cooking, and then divided the cleaning into tasks that they then assigned to each girl. Which was why Isla and Carina were out in the last of the light, with instructions to save the mallow roses from leafy intruders.

Carina tied the lavender ribbon into a bow so perfect it

looked out of a display window. "Eduarda likes me," she said, putting on pink garden gloves. "She says I remind her of herself when she was my age, and whenever you hear that, you know you can get anything you want. Well, anything she can get past her older sisters. That's why you and I are weeding together now, and that's why we'll be the ones slicing potatoes and soaking them before breakfast tomorrow. I told her I wanted to be put with you on chores as often as possible."

"Why?" Isla asked.

"Because of your sister," Carina said.

Isla's eyes crawled from the flower beds to Carina. "What about my sister?"

"Don't you know? She was royalty here." Carina sat down on her own dress, her skirt settling around her like a pink cloud. She didn't even seem to notice the graying dust from the fine gravel. "She was just one of those girls who seemed like she was born to be here. Like a statue of a Muse or something. So I thought being around you, some of that Soler enchantment might rub off on me."

What a disappointment Carina was in for. Though it did explain a lot. Isla had been tamping down a bristling of suspicion about why Carina was being so friendly. It had seemed like a trick, a setup. The truth was simpler and less sinister. Carina had adored Renata, just as so many adored Renata. And since Renata had graduated, Isla was as close to Renata as Carina could get.

Isla did not sit. Or kneel. She crouched and bent down to pull each weed. Abuela had asked the dress shop to send a wardrobe fit for a young lady to wear to tea, and Isla could tell just from the weave of the chiffon that they cost the earth. Isla hadn't been able to get out of Abuela exactly how much of the earth, but the sheer fact that Abuela wouldn't say told Isla everything.

"How long were you here with my sister?" Isla asked. She tried to sound as casual as her hands whispering among the satin flowers.

"Oh, not long." Carina's fingers wove deeper into the flower bed. "I just got here. By the time I unpacked my suitcases, Renata was a waltz away from graduating. But what I'm talking about, you don't need to know someone for long to know. She just had that kind of grace."

Carina went on. And on. Renata was as beautiful and skilled at etiquette and deportment as any finishing school had ever seen. Her movements were smooth as if she were moving through water. She looked flawless in true white, the brown of her skin and hair making her dress look like an azalea planted in the richest earth. She was as lovely as a doll, but sparkling and alive. She was elegant without being joyless, graceful without being restrained. She had the particular look that left a room fond with wonderstruck sighs.

Yes, Renata was that beautiful. She'd gotten love letters from boys and girls in town who'd never even met her, and who'd only seen her from across a street or heard her whispered name. Yes, she was sparkling and alive like that, but not once she came back from here.

Carina had caught a glimpse of some in-between Renata, someone between the sister Isla knew and the Alarie girl who came home. To Isla, Renata had been the sister who dragged her up into attics so they could try to tame the mice and use them to scare away anyone they didn't like. To Carina, Renata was lofty as a queen, observable but unknowable. And yet Carina knew more about who Renata was now than Isla did.

"I'm sorry." Carina drew her gloves up so they hovered over her mouth. "This is the worst, isn't it? Hearing how wonderful your sister is? I should know better. I have a prima like that. Everyone talks about her and I just want to scream."

Isla pulled a reedy stem from the velvet flowers. "If you just got here, how does Eduarda like you so much?"

"I win people over quickly. You'll see." Carina reached between the snapdragons. "So." She pulled a weed as quickly and ruthlessly as wringing the neck of a chicken. "What'd you do?"

Isla looked at her. "Excuse me?"

"Oh, I've heard all about you." Carina wove her hands between the poppies, translucent as tissue paper and paler than any Isla had seen at home. "You left. Now you're back."

So much for Luisa's fresh start. Maybe none of the same girls were here as the first time Isla had been enrolled, but gossip always had a way of filtering down through a place like this.

"And I'd bet my favorite shoes it's because someone in your family made you," Carina said. "Maybe you drank too much Prosecco at a fancy party and started dancing on the dessert table, macarons flying all over like confetti." She almost purred at the suggestion of scandal. "Or maybe you took a neighbor's shiny new motorcar out for a drive in the middle of the night, you know, just borrowing it, and drove it right into a pond, water lilies all over the dashboard."

"This level of detail makes me think *you've* done those things," Isla said. "Is that why you're here?"

"No." With her gloved palms, Carina urged an errant constellation of gravel back into place. "I'm here because I've wanted to be an Alarie girl since I was five years old. Other girls asked for dolls. I asked for the magazines with society photos."

Isla could see it, Carina tacking up glossy pages, Carina imitating the pictured poses and expressions. She would have acted out greeting an ambassador with lace-gloved hands. She would have imagined the silk of those socialites' voices. She would have imagined herself in a pink tulle gown and heavy emeralds at her throat so vividly she would have been able to feel the weight.

"And I'm going to enjoy every minute here, even the minutes when Alba's glaring at me for putting too many ribbons in my hair." Carina straightened up. "Your turn. How'd you end up back here?"

Isla looked right at her, the way Abuela might level a gaze at a rival. "I don't shake hands correctly."

"Fine." Carina adjusted the ribbon under her hat. "Don't tell me. But you will. You'll like me. Even if you don't want to." Carina got to her feet.

Isla stood up straight. "What is that supposed to mean?"

"You don't want to like me. I can tell." Carina gathered up the weeds they'd pulled. "Most people I meet either like me instantly or are determined not to. But they never last long."

SIXTEEN

THIS TIME, ISLA WAS going to be fearless. This time, she wasn't letting any of the Alarie girls scare her off.

And yet here she was, hiding behind a closed door.

As soon as the Alarie sisters had gone to bed, girls filled the halls, laughing and shoving perfume in each other's faces like the boys at school did with spiders. They changed in front of each other like it was nothing. They changed with their doors open. They were loose and relaxed with their own bodies, chattering while half-dressed, showing off new slips and bras like lace-adorned peacocks.

Every day, Isla did an artist's job of padding her own

brassiere, of choosing skirts and dresses that made her silhouette look a little more like Renata's. But the artistry required her to stay fully dressed. Brassieres even under her nightgowns.

"Isla." Carina's voice came with a delicate but persistent knock. "Come out here. Naomi has a bustier so complicated it should come with blueprints. You've never seen anything like it."

Girls at school had once declared Isla not one of them. Here, girls were inviting her into their filmy chaos, and Isla couldn't go near it. She felt so conspicuously, self-consciously dressed, as obvious as if she'd been wearing an overcoat indoors.

"What are you doing in there? Arranging hairpins?" Carina's knock turned into a string of knocks. "Stop being boring and come out here."

"Stop being annoying and leave her alone," a whisper in a different voice said. "She's probably asleep."

"I'm not annoying," Carina said, whispering now, as two sets of footsteps shuffled away from the door.

Isla waited until the hall went quiet, doors shut, lights out. She waited until they had all gone to bed, none of them going back and forth between their rooms and the bathroom sinks.

She snuck out of her room, brassiere on under her nightgown, shoes off. The heels Abuela had chosen for her, meant to help her blend in with the other girls, were oyster gray, stiff as a new book cover, and had already begun rubbing blisters on the edges of her toes.

The hall lamps had been turned low for the night. The chandelier barely cast enough light to reach down to the foyer tile and the offending crack. It hung just beyond the railing, anchored to the underside of the third floor where the Alarie sisters had their bedrooms. The tiers of jewels were lighter and translucent at the top. The bobeches holding the candle slips were watery blues and sherbet pinks.

All of it just hanging there, out in the open. The center column deepened into the teal of blue tourmaline, illuminated by jelly opals that glowed green from the inside. The gems were even richer lower down, as though color was collecting in the chandelier basket. Rubies hung alongside sapphires, and the freckled green of bloodstones looked frozen, filled with feathery white like the insides of ice cubes.

It was even more dazzling up close, like stained glass knocking around in a kaleidoscope.

It was so dazzling that it took Isla longer than it should have to notice the girl inside the chandelier.

She was sitting in the basket, holding two of the brass arms. Auburn hair half obscured her face. Her wraith-white nightgown ended in wisps like smoke.

This girl was hanging on the underside of the third floor. If she slipped out of the chandelier, she would fall two stories before landing.

Yet her posture was calm, her feet and the hem of her nightgown trailing down past the basket and finial. But her eyes were wide and staring, moving only as the chandelier gradually spun. She showed no fear, and no awareness of how far she might fall.

Isla looked around for a sign of anyone awake, any seam of light at the bottom of a door. When she turned toward one of the hallways branching off the mezzanine, her heart flinched in surprise, then relief. There was another girl, someone else up, someone else who could help get the girl in the chandelier down.

But Isla's heart didn't even have the chance to settle before she registered the familiar auburn hair, the pale nightgown, the dim sparkle of low-lit jewels. Isla was looking at a mirror, at the reflection of the girl in the chandelier. And the girl was smiling. No, not smiling. Not *just* smiling. Baring her teeth, which were sharp and translucent and glittering as the points of solitaire-cut diamonds. She did not snarl or hiss like an animal showing its incisors. The sound coming through the narrow space between her bared teeth was a pinched, airless scream.

A shudder went through Isla's chest. It whirled her around to face the actual girl with her cut-diamond teeth, instead of the terrifying reflection.

But the pinched scream cut out as though sealed in a jar.

The girl was gone.

The chandelier hung quiet.

Amethysts caught the light, the purple cut through with veining. Teardrop emeralds dangled within the crown. Pink tourmaline looked like a sunset caught within glass.

But there was no sign that a girl had been there. Nothing except the chandelier swinging lightly, as though a draft had just gone through.

SEVENTEEN

"**D**O THIS INEFFECTUALLY,**"** Alba Alarie said, "and you'll be closing your eyes against the light the entire conversation. Do it too vigorously, and it will seem as though you're criticizing your host for arranging an event outside on a bright day."

Depending on whom you asked, finishing school either taught the art of graces so small you might not otherwise consider them, or it taught girls to overthink everything.

"You may, of course, be right in your assessment of her scheduling," Alba said, "but these are thoughts to keep to yourself."

In this case, Alba had gathered the newer girls around

small white wrought iron tables for the purpose of teaching them exactly how to shade their eyes from the sun.

"Gently." Alba raised a white-gloved hand—she seemed too young to be wearing that style of glove, something from decades ago. "But decisively." Her fingers were lightly curved, like a dancer's in high fifth. "Thereby shielding your eyes without drawing too much attention to yourself."

Without drawing attention to yourself? The way Alba placed her hand near her forehead made her seem as though she might need a fainting couch at any moment.

"See over there?" Without breaking the artful curve of her fingers, Alba indicated another wrought iron table— white, round, just like the ones Isla and Carina and the rest of the newer girls were gathered around. But this one sat in the distance, closer to the house.

A group of older girls sat on matching white wrought iron chairs, dressed in shades of green so faint that Isla wasn't sure if they were really green or if it was a whisper of color reflected from the olive trees. They wore wide hats, trimmed with matching ribbons, but the two who were looking right into the sun shielded their eyes in perfect demonstration of Alba's technique.

Isla tried to make out the girls' faces. Two had reddish hair, shades that could have seemed auburn in low light. But she couldn't tell if either of them was the girl in the chandelier.

"They don't come to class?" Isla asked Carina when Alba was adjusting the line of a girl's arm.

"They're close to graduating," Carina whispered. "So you won't see them in lessons with the rest of us much, not unless they're asked to sit in and be good examples. They're mostly in tutorials, so instead of going to lectures, they're the ones setting the table displays before meals, arranging the flowers, learning patisserie in the kitchen. One day that'll be us. But for now, we're washing dishes, polishing silver, and proving we can be trusted not be embarrass anyone with too great a faux pas."

Isla watched them, transfixed. Not because they were almost as beautiful as Renata. Not even because they made up their own closed world. But because they looked so serenely sure of each gesture, each tilt of a chin, each lift of a napkin to the corner of a mouth, each light touch from one girl to another to underscore a joke. What was it like to be that sure of yourself as a girl, to not even have to think about it?

When Alba dismissed the class, girls streamed between the house and the gardens. A few clustered together. One walked with her arm around another's waist, both leaning their heads in. Their hair, in different shades of brown, and skirts, in identical shades of white, pressed together.

"Gianna, Bernarda," Alba said as she strode by them. "We've discussed this. No exuberant displays of affection in public." She didn't even slow her pace to give the correction. "It is in bad taste. We are not lesbians."

"Maybe *they're* not." A familiar voice passed behind Isla. It came with the faint smell of white azalea, and it was so perfectly calibrated that Alba didn't even hear Paz.

Alba went on toward the house, greeting Paz as they fell in step together. She didn't even realize Paz had just spoken behind her back.

Isla passed the table with the gently laughing girls. She passed with enough distance that she could make it seem accidental, a matter of gravity, but close enough to try to get a better look at their faces.

"Isla, isn't it?" A blonde lifted her head and also a lace-gloved hand, as though summoning a waiter.

Isla stopped.

"Join us," another said, pushing a vacant chair out with her dainty heel. She had her dark hair pulled into the kind of bun that should have looked stuffy but that instead looked fresh and neat, like she was vacationing and just wanted her hair out of her face.

"We don't bite," a third said, still waiting for Isla to sit. "Unless we've skipped lunch."

Isla sat. Few things seemed more conspicuous here than refusing the invitation of more experienced Alarie girls. There was something commanding about them. Not forceful. Not even intimidating, not exactly. More as though you would be going against the natural order of the cosmos if you did not give them what they wanted. Ignore one's request, and the earth's magnetic field might be in peril. Turn away from their bid for conversation, and the sun might throw off a solar flare.

"We must tell you," one girl said.

"We simply love your sister," a second said.

"Adore her," a third added.

"Will she be visiting?" a fourth asked, inclining slightly forward.

The faces around the table all looked at Isla hopefully.

At their inquiring expressions, a realization buckled in Isla's stomach. She couldn't ask where they thought Renata might have gone, not without the risk of them guessing that she'd vanished. Isla would have bet Renata's ring that she'd learn more by watching and listening than by asking these girls outright. That was the way of finishing school girls, everything subtle, circuitous, understated. Address anything too directly, and they withdrew.

"If she can get away, she will." Isla heard herself imitating the bell-like voices of these girls. "I'm dizzy just thinking about her schedule."

"Oh?" the blonde asked, her eyes opening wider with interest, enough that Isla could see they were brown, not blue. "What is she up to these days?"

She said it with such pure interest that Isla didn't even think she was fishing for gossip. None of these expectant faces seemed to know that Renata Soler, the shining finishing school graduate, had vanished out a window in the middle of the night.

"She's so busy preparing for the upcoming season," Isla said. "Visits to dressmakers, arrangements with hotels, making acquaintances with family friends. You know how it is."

The girls hummed in understanding. They lifted and lowered sympathetic chins, affirming that, yes, they all, in fact, *knew how it was.*

Isla glanced around at the faces. There were three redheads. None of them looked like the girl in the chandelier, or rather, all of them looked as much like her as the others. Copper-haired, skin so pale it would have looked white if they weren't sitting on white furniture. Watching eyes that were different colors—one girl's hazel, one blue, one brown.

The difference in color told Isla nothing. The girl in the chandelier had eyes so wide that her pupils had taken up most of the irises. It could have been any of the three of them, or none of them. Isla wouldn't know unless the right girl stared at her, unblinking, and bared her teeth.

That night, Isla looked for the girl in the chandelier again. Once she heard the doors shut and the laughter quiet, she stepped into the dim hall.

The chandelier was empty.

She moved along the mezzanine railing, looking for movement, a sign that someone had climbed out of it.

As light glanced off the tiers, a sound drifted through the air like a draft.

Everything's here.

The whisper seemed to come from the walls.

But even in a whisper, Isla recognized the voice.

"Renata?" Isla looked around, the name coming out faint as a breath.

No one was there. But she knew she'd heard it, as though the sound was woven into the wallpaper.

Everything a girl like you needs. Renata's whisper rippled gently through the air. *Everything girls like us could want.*

Either Isla was falling into the same madness as Renata, or she was closer to finding her.

EIGHTEEN

ON EACH DESK IN the library waited a set of paper dolls.

Isla tried to keep her stomach from bucking, remembering those nauseating lessons in school, also with paper dolls. *This is what makes a girl. This is what makes a boy.* The girls in Isla's class saying, *Here, you really need this one for you,* and handing her a badly drawn, badly cut-out rendering of a cow.

Their teacher back then, a kind, damp-eyed young woman who was probably not much older than Isla was now, had been perplexed. Isla had the same soft body as so many other girls in the class. It was an age where some girls were spindly as celery stalks and others still had grasa parda. Why would they be calling Isla chubby?

That poor teacher hadn't understood the insult. The vicious artistry of Isla's classmates had gone completely over her head. It had nothing to do with weight and everything to do with a very specific fact about cows.

"Ladies, take your seats," Alba said. "Though it may appear as though we're about to play with toys, I assure you, we have much to cover."

But the dolls in the Alarie House library were not the round, pigtailed ones from children's books. These ladies were grown, tall, and of course, lily-reed thin, with coiffed blond hair, green eyes, and peach complexions. They each stood in demure, proper posture.

Carina held up one of the plain dolls, which didn't look so much naked as blank. The figure's anatomy cut off with dotted lines at the upper arms and thighs. The body within those bounds was empty white paper.

"Hmm." Carina turned it over and then back. "Reminds me of reproductive education at my school."

Isla had been holding her throat so tightly that when she laughed she almost choked on it.

As they sat down at adjacent desks, Isla took in the rest of the paper pieces. Alongside each flat woman was a whole flat wardrobe. Paper dresses and skirts in different colors and drawn fabrics, paper shoes of all styles, even paper parasols.

Alba strode to the front of the library. As ever, she matched the stones on her neck. Another purple dress, this one more lilac, picked up the warmer tones in the amethysts.

"Shall we begin by dressing our ladies for a morning visit?" she asked.

As Isla and Carina reached for cutouts of pastel dresses, Paz slipped into the vacant desk on the other side of Isla. She did it so fluidly she seemed liquid, a cat slipping into a basket.

"And I certainly hope our paper lady is more prompt than some." Alba didn't even say it under her breath. She said it quietly but crisply, and it carried across the library.

"My apologies." Paz shrugged and sank into her seat. Even she wasn't immune to the withering critique of the Alarie sisters.

Carina folded the paper flaps onto the doll's shoulders. "Careful," she whispered.

"What does that mean?" Isla whispered back.

Alba paused over a girl's desk. "An evening gown. What an interesting choice. Perhaps she'd also like to attend a ball in a house skirt to even things out?"

Carina added light blue paper shoes. "I think you have a suitor."

In infinitesimal increments, Isla scooted her chair closer to Carina's and away from Paz's. "I think I have someone who's bored." Paz had practically said as much the first time they met.

Carina's shrug seemed an entirely different gesture than Paz's. Paz's had been loose and slouching. Carina's was delicate and precise as the flick of a wrist. "She sat next to you at breakfast too."

"So did you," Isla whispered.

Carina's mouth quirked into a smile. "Then I'm very sorry to dash your hopes, because you're not my type."

"I'm sure I'll learn to love again," Isla said in a passionate whisper.

"Stop." Carina pressed her lips together to keep from laughing. "You're going to make her jealous."

Was this the wondrous power of the Alarie House? Carina was exactly the kind of pretty, frilly, pink-wearing girl that had once scorned Isla. And here she was sitting next to her, both of them trying not to get caught laughing.

Renata hadn't needed that. She'd always made friends quickly and easily. Isla's friends back home had been Renata's friends first. So what had made Renata stay here? What was so alluring here that she'd never found anywhere else?

Alba cast her voice over the library. "And what might our lady wear if she'd like to take in a spring afternoon, but there seems to be a chance of rain?"

That one even Isla knew. Avoid the white dresses, unless the paper woman wanted to be accused of displaying herself in sheer wet linen.

"Girls have been caught with girls before," Carina whispered. "Les demoiselles don't treat it any differently than being caught in your room with a boy."

"Now let's clothe our ladies for"—Alba took a few steps down the aisle between desks, considering—"a day of walking and shopping in town."

Carina leaned closer. "If their apologies are absolute

works of art, they get to stay, but they'll be shining the copper pots after dinner for the next month. If their groveling is lackluster, they get sent home."

Alba stood over another girl. "Bright colors in the street? No, my dear, here we must favor understated tones."

"Of course it's far too scandalous of a matter to actually speak of, whether she's caught with a boy or another girl." Carina shuffled paper dresses like cards. "So they never tell the parents what happened. They simply say something like *Your daughter is not a good fit for our course of instruction.* Which, personally, I'd rather everyone know I was caught in a compromising position than have les demoiselles tell my family I'm not Alarie House material. Can you imagine? I'd rather die."

Alba turned her attention to another girl's work. "Don't we think that lace might suffer in the crush of the crowds? Let's try a heartier fabric."

Isla removed the lace parasol she'd fastened to her paper doll's hand.

"Remember, ladies," Alba said, "it's vulgar to wear an expensive dress out in the lane. Keep this in mind for our lady's next occasion, which will be traveling."

Isla reached for a paper coat.

Carina feigned a cough, knocked it away from Isla's fingers and tapped another one.

Isla fastened the different coat onto her paper woman.

"Carina, dear, there's no valor in fracturing a rib suppressing a cough," Alba said. "And there's no shame in excusing yourself from the room and returning once the spell has passed." As Alba walked, the rolled hem of her skirt flowed ahead of her. "Let us not forget our lady will need sturdy boots and gloves."

Isla felt Paz looking at her. Pretending to reach for a paper garment on the corner of her desk, Isla took Paz into her peripheral vision.

"And how might our lady adorn her hair for a party?" Alba asked. Almost immediately, she stopped over a girl's desk. "Feathers? Truly? Do we mean to turn her into a cabaret performer?"

Carina grabbed a few paper wisps of ribbon and lace.

Isla reached for the jeweled crescent moon of a thin tiara.

Carina shook her head.

Isla reached for an arc of flowers.

Carina nodded.

"If you know all this already," Isla whispered, "why are you here?"

"You really don't get it, do you?" Carina said, though her tone was humoring. "The particulars are just the beginning. Being an Alarie girl is not just about what you do, but about how you do it. It's about the grace with which you move through the world."

"Maybe you should be teaching here," Isla whispered.

"No one teaches here unless they come directly from the Alarie family." Carina said as they attached the adornments to the paper women's hair. "For generations back. Can you imagine being born with that kind of glamour in your blood?"

Paz's hand flashed at the corner of Isla's desk, quick as a magician's. Her fingers left behind a small green gem, cut into the smooth oval of a cabochon.

"Peridot," Paz said, not whispering, simply lowering her voice as quiet as it went.

"Or evening emerald." Paz didn't even try to hide talking to Isla. She wasn't fiddling with the paper dolls or feigning staring at her desk. "That's what some lapidaries call it."

Her voice brushed against the back of Isla's neck.

"What did I tell you?" Carina whispered. "Now she's giving you jewels."

The green of the peridot glowed faintly, like the last afternoon light on grass.

"They form beneath the earth's crust," Paz said. "And they need the fire of magma to bring them to the surface, just like diamonds."

Alba stopped between Isla's desk and Paz's.

Isla braced for a lecture on talking during class.

"Let us treat our wardrobe more gently, shall we?" Alba said.

Isla realized she was crunching a paper dress between her fingers.

"After all"—Alba turned to the rest of the room—"the most beautiful garment loses its charm with a bent collar or ripped lace."

Isla gave up her grip on the paper.

Alba strolled back to the front of the library. "And remember the old saying, 'A lady is most elegantly dressed when you cannot remember what she wore.'"

As Alba turned her back, Isla breathed out.

Paz was beautiful, and she had a voice as rich as the evergreens outside. There was something both pretty and boyish about her, the brazenness of a girl who had grown up with only brothers and who wouldn't have had it any other way.

And Isla hated her a little for it, for being so sure of herself. Not in the soft, gracious way the older girls were sure of themselves. Paz moved through the world like she was looking to scandalize people.

At Alba's next instruction, Isla looked down at the paper doll.

The doll's hair had deepened to black. Her fair skin had turned light brown, her green eyes now dark. And Isla had the odd sense that the doll was looking at her. No, not just looking at her. Smiling at her.

With a hitch of panic, Isla checked Carina's paper doll. Then Paz's. And everyone else's she could see. But they were all the same, pale, blond, green-eyed. And by the time Isla looked back at her desk, so was her own. Her paper doll was as it had been when she first sat down. Except for the quirk of her smile as she looked back at Isla.

NINETEEN

IN HER NIGHTMARES, HER heart froze into a garnet. First, it was a glowing rough, then sheared away, cut into facets. Then it glittered under glass where she could not get to it. It pulsed with the faint, beating whisper of words Isla could not make out.

She needed it, the raw muscle of her heart, the mineral replica it had become, the words that could have been words Renata wanted her to hear. Without them, she was hollow. Without them, she was no more a living thing than the glass she was banging her hands against.

She jammed the heels of her hands into it, but the glass was already different than it had been a minute ago. It was no longer a jewelry case, edged in gold. Instead, the glass was the floor underneath her. She threw her fists into it, and it would not give.

Until it did. The glass splintered like an ice cube buckling in hot water.

She was about to plunge her hands through and put her fingers around her own heart. But then the glass turned to tile.

Isla woke up kneeling in the sunken atrium, in the Alarie House. It wasn't her hands breaking things apart. She was driving the heel of an oyster-gray pump into the crack she'd left in the tile. And the crack was spreading.

Isla stopped her hands. She made them stop even though she could barely feel them. She could barely feel the broken nails or bleeding cuticles or split knuckles.

She sensed the prickling of eyes watching. She heard their laughter, light as the heads of primroses bobbing in the night breeze.

They were all looking at her, and they could all see inside her, down to her cells. They would revile her as deeply as the girls in grade school had. The boys had reviled her too, but she had never been afraid of the boys the way she had of the girls.

Girls knew how to wound quietly, without anyone noticing. They knew how to wield whispers and rumors. They knew how to craft insults so perfect they became indelible. They didn't even need words. They could do it with a glance.

They had seen that something was wrong with Isla. And

now all the exceptional young ladies waltzing and bowing their way toward Alarie approval had seen it too.

Isla let go of the shoe. It fell onto its side on the cracking tile. There would be no sweeping this away a second time. She had damaged this priceless house not once but twice. The staring girls would have to tell the Alarie sisters. The Alarie sisters would have to hold her to account.

But when Isla looked up, there was no one on the mezzanine. No girls in pale nightgowns stood at the railings.

The laughter still clung to the air. It wasn't in her dream. It was real and it was coming from above her, as though it was radiating from the chandelier itself.

Isla crept up the staircase, the laughter shivering over her back. But then she was on the landing, almost level with the chandelier, and the laughing still seemed higher, as though the voices were coming from the ceiling.

Or the third floor.

It wasn't the Alarie sisters. It couldn't be. The voices were too high and too numerous. They fizzed over one another, the bubbling mirth of a dozen or more girls, not three distinguished Señoras running a finishing school.

Isla took slow steps down the hall, the jewels winking as she passed. The deep green of the trees filled the windows, and the blue of the night made their gently rustling branches look like a dark, vertical sea, waves rippling in front of the glass.

Isla listened to those voices. She shut her eyes and found

the thread of them. This was chilling, defiant glee. This was the wild, reckless laughter of girls who might be cackling while holding blood-covered knives over their finishing school instructors. If Isla caught them in the act, her own blood might be the second coat.

But the farther down the hallway she went, the more the voices sounded hollow and distant, as though they were behind the walls.

Isla paused before the stairwell to the third floor. Just like the wide staircase from the foyer, there were gems embedded into the walls. The stairs were the same richly finished wood.

The similarities stopped there. This stairwell was narrow, barely lit, without flocked wallpaper or scrolled banisters. The jewels in the walls were small and sparse enough to look like distant constellations, and with so little light, the gold settings barely gleamed.

Isla tracked the direction of the sound. It wasn't coming from the third floor. It was more directly above. It sounded like it was coming from the roof.

Renata's lessons on sneaking out kicked in like muscle memory. Slowly, moving the sash so gradually it wouldn't make noise, Isla opened a window. She threw one leg over. If she anchored herself properly, she'd be able to see the roof from here.

Then the first hand reached out of the dark.

TWENTY

THE HAND GRABBED ISLA'S arm as hard as if its fingers were teeth. She could not turn to see the girl it belonged to. She could see only up to the girl's elbow. The brown of the forearm made the ruffled sleeve so starkly white it looked made of moonlight.

Isla resisted the grip. But a matching hand appeared, and they were pulling Isla off the windowsill.

She tried to twist out of their hold, but they were winning, and she was out in the night air. The tiled roof loomed over her. Bougainvillea and morning glories spilled off the edges, not the deep pink and bright purple of the ones along the front of the house. These were all white, ghostly among the green leaves.

A white bougainvillea bloom drifted down toward the ground. Her body would follow.

More hands came out of the dark. They descended from above, joining in the work of throwing her to the ground. The more she fought them, the more hands appeared.

An arm wrapped around her waist. It drew her up. It didn't let her go, as though wanting to make her guess when she'd fall.

Then, with the help of the other hands, it pulled her up and onto an eave.

She was not falling.

She was standing on the lowest stretch of the roof.

And she was facing Paz, the one to whom that first hand, that forearm, that fluttering white sleeve, belonged.

Out here, with no light but the garden lamps below and the silver of the stars, Paz's hair was a true enough shade of black that it was closer to blue than brown. It matched her pants, both them and her hair a perfect contrast against the white of her dressing gown. Her hair draped over her shoulders in imitation of the robe's ruffled edging. She looked like she should be holding a candle and walking through a Victorian novel.

A sapphire winked between the frilled panels of Paz's collar, and Paz caught her looking.

"Like it?" She lifted it away from her throat. "It has rather unusual dichroism, quite distinct along one axis. Not unlike rubies that are pink three ways and orange the fourth." As Paz moved it, the sapphire seemed to take in all the light from the sky above them. It shone different blues, first lighter like cornflowers, then darker like the sea, before it flashed purple.

Girls in their pale nightgowns milled away from Paz, as though resuming previous activities. One smiled at Isla and said, "Welcome," but the rest weren't really paying attention to Isla or to Paz. They had just helped pull Isla up, and they had done it with the efficiency and skill that spoke of how often they'd done it before.

The girls were walking up the rise of the roof, to where it crested above the third floor.

They were walking on the heads of the sleeping Alarie sisters.

And they were walking three stories above the ground, with the carefree steps of spinning through a meadow. A few twirled along the roofline, arms out like some adored company of tightrope walkers. Some danced along the edge of the roof, so close that the breeze swept their hair out over the three-story drop.

Isla's body still hadn't settled, but there was room for new fear. It trembled through her, the possibility that this was some kind of terrifying initiation.

Yet none of the older girls seemed to be pushing or pulling anyone toward the edge. A cluster of younger girls sat on the roof, arms around their knees as they watched, and everyone seemed to leave them alone except for greeting them as they passed.

When girls did draw each other toward the edges, it was with nothing but laughing voices and beckoning hands. No pushing. No pulling on arms.

A yellow nightgown made Isla turn her head. Carina stood watching everyone, and when she realized Isla was watching her, she looked back, smiling and thrilled.

"What are they doing?" Isla breathed out the question to no one in particular. But it was Paz who was close enough to hear it, and Paz who answered.

"Reckless things that proper Alarie girls would never do, of course."

The distant thrill in Paz's voice spoke of feeling apart from these girls. She watched them. She observed them. And she seemed to feel even less like one of them than Isla.

Carina drifted past Isla, toward the edge of an eave.

"Carina," Isla said.

Carina paused, her round eyes wide and blinking.

"What are you doing?" Isla asked.

Exhilaration lit Carina's face. "How can we be diamonds if we're afraid to get scratched?"

Carina turned, her hair almost blond from the moon and the shine of the roof tiles.

"Carina," Isla called after her.

But then another girl passed.

Isla knew that hair, the dark brown waves loose and long. Even from the back, Isla recognized the shoulders, the cant of the wrist, always a little tilted up, like some old painting of a maiden wandering into a forest. She knew that walk, fearless but full of wonder, as though some exciting magic waited a few steps in front of her.

"Renata?"

But the girl kept going toward the edge of the roof.

"Renata." Isla grasped her arm to stop her.

The girl whirled around, the face different.

The similarity vanished, replaced by startled eyes, wide and bathwater blue instead of her sister's dark, impish gaze.

Not-Renata's hair blew into her alarmed face.

In the same instant, half the girls on the roof started screaming. It was a fractured, breaking sound, a raw, blood-chilling scream, but with a core like the awful ringing of a finger circling the wet edge of a wineglass. They screamed, and their back teeth glinted like cut diamonds. They screamed, and their faces splintered apart into facets. They screamed, and their features refracted away from their faces, like light bouncing through a cut jewel.

Isla let her go.

The screaming stopped.

The light settled, and the girls whose faces were dividing into facets came back together. Their smiles were placid as the shine off polished silver. Including not-Renata, who amiably nodded in greeting, as though pleased to make Isla's acquaintance, before going on her way.

The girls who had not screamed now stared, though not in horror. More like they were marveling. They gazed at the older girls as though they had done a party trick they would give anything to learn.

The ringing echoed in Isla's head. It banged through her like a solid object. She couldn't even summon a smile to give back to the girls who were smiling so sympathetically at her, as though she had made nothing more than an honest mistake. It was an error as understandable as placing a napkin on a chair instead of the table, their tilting heads told Isla. Anyone could have done the same, their gracious faces declared.

"You're a kind heart to care so much," said one of the older girls who'd asked after Renata. "But there was no need to worry for her. There's no need to worry for any of us. Real jewels don't break when they fall." She said it with the calming sureness of telling a little sister there were no ghosts in the closet.

"It's okay," a girl with strawberry-blond hair and large brown eyes said. "If you're not ready."

"But when you know you're a true gem, you will be," another said, this one with dark hair straight as the edge of a dinner knife. The light blue band of a perfectly placed ribbon crossed her head. "When you know that nothing but another diamond can touch you, you will be."

The girl said it with such gentle conviction that Isla could feel the words on her skin. Not like the words she'd been called when she was younger. This almost sounded like a blessing. And Isla wanted it. She wanted the certainty that these girls carried with them to dining room tables and to the edges of roofs.

But the screaming still rang through Isla. And it had to be ringing down through the house. Any moment, an Alarie sister would be leaning out a window demanding to know what, in heaven's name, was going on up there.

"We're going to get caught," Isla said, to all of them at once. But they were back to their dances along the rooflines.

"They can't hear us," Paz said.

Isla thought she was talking about the other girls, until she noticed Paz looking down at her feet, toward the third floor. "They never do."

TWENTY-ONE

"**L**OVELY POSTURE, MAURICIA.**" Luisa Alarie's resonant voice flowed down the breakfast table. Her dress matched the blue in the dining room windows. "Ladies, observe the elegance of your fellow classmate on this beautiful morning."

Nothing seemed quite real at the Alarie House. Not the air that was so dustless Isla couldn't even find motes drifting through the sunbeams. Not the baseboards that never showed a single scuff.

Not the crack in the foyer floor that was starting to seem as though it had always been there.

"She is motionless without appearing rigid or stiff," Luisa said.

Not the night before, girls twirling on their toes over roof tiles.

"That is the true art of comportment."

Mauricia stirred sugar into her tea, so placid she barely seemed to register the compliment. Her modesty seemed so complete it couldn't have been faked.

"Learning to be relaxed without being mistaken for a statue."

Not even the fruit here seemed real. The apples and pears in their pewter bowls looked painted pink and golden yellow. Tiny points of condensation glossed the peels like glass beads. And everyone's dresses looked fresh as buttercups, their jewelry little more than whispers of silver.

"Rocio," Alba said. "Speak up. Your companions can't hear you if you mumble. Mumbling is little better than shouting. Viviana, we've discussed this. Put the book away. Hiding it on your lap is not as subtle as you think."

Paz offered Isla the berry preserves. "Confiture?" It looked like a bowl of clotted blood.

Paz's white shirt was crisp as the tablecloth, her ironed trousers neatly tucked into her boots, braid tied with a ribbon. The way she leaned a little forward, one palm on one knee, the other forearm resting on her other leg, made her look like a painted portrait. Her expression matched, the pride of a slightly lifted chin. Isla could imagine her descending a staircase or standing against a balustrade at dawn.

She got away with it too, sitting like that at breakfast. She seemed so attuned to the Alarie sisters' attention that every time either one of them looked her way, she adjusted her position.

Isla wasn't letting this girl or anyone else unsettle her. If she looked uncomfortable, someone might start wondering why.

She looked Paz right in the eye with a ladylike, "Thank you." She took a spoonful of the dark red, catching a preserved strawberry in the curve.

She knocked it directly onto her plate, no bread, just blood on porcelain like a miniature heart.

Carina lowered herself into the chair next to Isla. Her skirt puffed around her like pink frosting.

She chirped, "Morning," looking fresh as if she'd been sleeping since early the previous evening.

"*Good* morning," Luisa said. "It contributes nothing to rapport or to conversation to simply state the time of day."

Carina sighed so lightly Isla was probably the only one to hear it. "And there's my allotted error for the next twenty-four hours," she whispered, pulling her chair in. "Pity. I don't usually burn through it that quickly."

As Eduarda told a group of older girls to bring formal heels to their morning tutorial, Isla leaned closer to Carina. "What was all that last night?"

Carina blinked, tilting her head at the same angle that she paused her spoon. "What was what?"

"Everything on the roof," Isla whispered.

Carina's face furrowed into a confused pinch that must have been adorable to anyone who ever fell in love with her. But right now, it was just annoying.

That was it? A puzzled look?

No *I know, wasn't it the strangest thing? I don't know what got into me.*

No *I was sure we were going to get caught. Wasn't it a thrill when we weren't?*

Not even *Wasn't it marvelous? You could see all the way to the mountains from up there.*

Not even a breathless rush that the older Alarie girls, these girls Carina had admired since she first read about this place in magazines, had included her in their nighttime games.

Carina just kept looking at Isla as though she didn't understand the question.

"You're on a fool's errand," Paz said, each word punctuated by cracking a spoon against the shell of a soft-boiled egg. "They'll never talk about it." Paz didn't lean toward Isla the way Isla and Carina leaned in to talk to each other. She kept her posture exactly as it was. "Alarie girls never talk about anything so unpleasant as making spectacles of themselves."

Isla's first instinct was to ignore Paz, her calm, secretive stare, the peridot that glowed green even at night. But Paz was the one person who seemed to notice that something was a little off with these sparkling young ladies. They seemed so tightly wound, so set on the work of being proper finishing school girls, that it left them a little delirious. Was this what had happened to Renata? Had she thrown herself into it so completely that it left her fevered?

Paz took a magenta apple from the bowl and held it toward Isla. "Would you like me to peel one for you?"

"No, thank you," Isla said.

"Are you sure?" Paz set the edge of a knife against the apple. "I'm very good at it. I can turn the whole thing into one ribbon. It's one of my best tricks."

Carina inclined her body toward Isla's on the premise of reaching for the sugar. "Sip your water and act like we're talking about the weather."

Coyness about the roof aside, Carina had yet to steer Isla wrong at the dining room table. So Isla pointedly mused at the brilliant blue and the spun-sugar clouds out the windows.

"You were right the first time," Carina said. "If you had an injured finger or generally had trouble with your hands, her offer would be a polite one. Nothing untoward about it, and nothing untoward in accepting. But if you have no difficulty with your hands and you let her—or worse, a man—peel fruit for you, it's an invitation."

"To what?" Isla asked.

Carina meaningfully widened her eyes at her napkin, as though summoning her patience with Isla, or trying not to blush at a scandal. "You might as well lie down right here on the lace tablecloth and invite her to put her head up your skirt."

With a slow turn, Isla told Paz, "No, thank you." She took a yellow apple from the pewter bowl. "I like to eat the peel."

She kept a defiant gaze on Paz as she drew it toward her mouth.

The moment before she bit into it, a hand flew through the space in front of her. Isla saw a blond head, an ice-green ribbon, the pale column of a toile dress, mint green on white.

As the moment stretched and frayed, Isla's fear was so familiar it was almost calming. It was the thrill of the inevitable. She had always known it was going to be this way. Adored girls turned on her. It was simply how things went. The only question would be when and how.

The when was becoming increasingly clear by the split second.

All that was left to know was whether that hand would go for Isla's face or her throat.

But the hand did not strike her. It did not grab her. The hand knocked the apple from Isla's grasp, and the apple sailed across the room.

One of the older girls, the blonde who had first invited Isla to sit with them in the garden, was on her feet. She had just reached across the table, so quickly it had taken Isla a few seconds to place which blonde had done it.

Isla stared at the standing girl, whose eyes were wide and unblinking. Her face held that same relentless sympathy Isla had seen last night on the roof.

"A lady," the girl said, with the slightest shake of her head, "never bites into fruit."

The Alarie sisters all dipped their heads as though to say *wise words* before returning to their breakfasts.

The girls around the table hummed their agreement, and then did the same.

The girl's face was the picture of understanding. She gave Isla a gracious little smile that seemed to say, *You're welcome, no need to thank me, we're all learning together.*

The apple settled on the dining room rug, a sad yellow-green planet listing on the axis of its stem.

Isla looked down the table at Mauricia. She was beautiful and blank as an unfinished painting, one in which the artist hadn't yet attended to the subject's eyes.

Two impulses blew through Isla like blasts of cold air.

First, she wanted to take their sympathy, their under-standing, their inclusion of her. She wanted to fold it up into a locket and keep it close. She wanted to wear it as proof of something.

But the second impulse pushed up against the first.

She wanted to know what might alarm these girls. She wanted to know what they might acknowledge as out of the ordinary.

Isla saw her hand grabbing the fruit knife. She saw her hand raising it up, driving it down through the air, plunging it into the table.

The second the point of the blade cut through the table-cloth and staked into the wood, she couldn't believe she'd done it. The knife vibrated, a mirror of Isla's breath shuddering in her chest. What had she been thinking? The Isla of a moment earlier was already a stranger to her.

The Alarie sisters would have to send her home for good. She'd leave knowing nothing, understanding nothing.

The newest girls were looking up, wide-eyed as startled cats.

But no one else did.

The newer ones looked around at the other girls and the Alarie sisters, all of them going on with their breakfast. This seemed to reassure them. They calmed and did the same. Even Carina only looked up for a minute, regarded the knife, and then seemed placated, as though knowing the source of the noise made it unremarkable.

"Isla, dear," Eduarda said. "Should you find yourself frightened by a spider at the breakfast table, there are far less disruptive ways to address the disturbance."

She didn't sound angry, or even as though she was warning Isla. Isla had just stabbed a knife into their dining room table, and Eduarda had the tone of kindhearted advice.

"Luisa once had a mouse crawl into her purse at the opera." Alba barely glanced up from the careful dissection of her breakfast. "And no one was the wiser, not even when she discovered it between acts."

If they wanted to, they could ignore anything.

Renata could have been unraveling here, and everyone would have missed it.

TWENTY-TWO

"**D**O NOT COVER YOUR** face when you laugh, Viviana. It makes you look as though you're snickering behind the backs of your companions."

"Rocio, there is no need to raise your voice when speaking to the young lady next to you. Only your conversation partner need hear you, not the entire room."

"Ladies, may I remind you to sit at the table with grace and dignity. Not so close as to restrict ease of movement. Not so far back that you'll be carrying your food right over your dress."

"Do not shred your roll into your soup, Gianna. And I've seen more than a few of you engaging in the awful habit of biting your bread. Must we review again how to break off small pieces?"

"Isla, do not swing your neck about. A loose neck is the sign of a loose woman."

Every meal, lesson, tea, and lecture was an onslaught of correction. And these girls, with their cheeks flushed peach, their dresses in the demure shades of ducks' eggs, took it as though they barely felt it. Even the newest girls didn't cower in their chairs under a correction. They held themselves straighter, as though they'd just received the attention of a ballet mistress.

Renata would have been the first to talk back. *I like my neck loose; perhaps you've overtightened yours. And are you impuning the virtue of swans?* If she'd graduated, then something here was worth holding her tongue.

"The spoon is for liquids, Beth. For anything else, employ the fork."

"Need I remind you all that nothing should be eaten with the hands except bread and fruit."

"No blowing on your tea, Naomi. Or your soup for that matter. Wait for it to cool. A lady never gives the appearance of being in a rush."

"For goodness' sake, Paz, stop slouching. You know better. You look like you're in a gambling hall."

"Isla, rest your knife and fork on your plate. If you hold them upright that way, your table companions are apt to think that at any moment you might launch yourself out of your chair to consume them."

Here, pointing out flaws was a blood sport.

And yet, no one said anything about that widening crack in the tile.

Girls walked over it as though it was nothing. The Alarie sisters didn't even seem to notice it. Their ignorance was so complete that Isla began to wonder if she was exaggerating the whole thing.

Maybe her on-edge mind had turned a chip or scratch into a crack. Maybe she had never really damaged it at all. The ground shifted, didn't it? Cracks appeared in floors. Maybe it was pure arrogance to think she could do anything to this spectacular house.

She kept going back to the foyer and staring down at it, and every time, there it was. There was something almost beautiful in how the crack threw the painted jewels a little off-kilter, as though they were being refracted through a water glass.

"My goodness." Alba Alarie's voice startled Isla into taking a step forward, closer to the first tiled stair down to the sunken atrium. "You look like you have a lot on your mind."

Isla needed something to cover this over, to show she wasn't dwelling on such a small thing, better ignored. She'd been staring at the crack in the tile so intently she might as well have needlepointed a pillow stitched with the words *I, Isla Soler, have marred your atrium floor.*

She went back to Renata's counsel. Weave truth in with your lies; better yet, weave as few lies as possible in with your truth.

Isla picked up a question she'd kept turning over in her

mind and then setting down, like the blown-glass paper-weight Luisa used during letter-writing lessons.

"I was just wondering if I missed something," Isla said.

Alba's frown was kind, almost sympathetic. She seemed in a good mood. She must have dreamed of perfectly ironed tablecloths last night. "What would you have missed?"

Isla looked at the girls moving from the library out toward the gardens. "Everyone here wears light colors, and I'm assuming that's because they're most appropriate to the season and to our age."

All Isla had done was quote that afternoon's lesson, but Alba looked pleased. She gave a little nod of *yes, go on*.

"Some girls wear all white though," Isla said. "And I can't figure out why. It's not based on how long they've been here. Some of the older girls still wear pastels. Some of the newer girls wear white and nothing else."

"Very astute." Alba lifted a gloved hand, fingers curled except for the index pointing heavenward. "A girl can never be too observant. A lady who observes is a lady who remembers names, occasions, and acquaintances." She lowered the angle of her hand, and now looked as though she was giving lessons to the air. "All white dress is not required. It's up to every girl how much she embraces the process. A cultured young lady pays eternal attention to detail," Alba said with the nod of a patient governess. "And keeping a white dress pristine requires unceasing attention to detail. It's excellent training. It's the same reason we give our girls black velvet gowns upon their commencement. Both require sureness and fastidious care. Only a girl with complete poise is ready to spoon preserves while donning a white tea dress, and only a girl who has certainty in herself can confidently attend a dinner party in a black velvet gown when the hosts might serve powdered-sugar desserts."

Isla could see it now, the scandal of fluffy white dusting the elegant black of plush velvet. She could imagine some poor girl trying to brush it away but spreading it instead, trying to clean it off with soda water but making the problem worse.

One of the older girls across the foyer lifted a pale hand in greeting. She seemed to be waving to Isla more than Alba, especially because she gave Alba a separate, deferential little bow.

"I know you were off to a difficult start here," Alba said, "but you seem to be getting on well."

As though on cue, another girl gave Isla a delicate wave.

"And you certainly seem to be fitting in nicely." Alba turned to look right at Isla, hands clasped in front of her as though she were about to break into an aria. "Commit yourself to the process, and you'll have your black velvet dress in no time."

Maybe it was Alba's words that Isla had to thank. Maybe there was magic in the voices of the Alarie sisters. But that night, the dark of her dreams had a new texture. It was the billowing velvet of a bona fide Alarie girl's perfect black dress.

This time, Isla's heart was a fire opal under a sheet of ice. She was jamming the point of a crystal into it. The ice was just beginning to give, just beginning to splinter, when she startled awake.

The crystal point turned to a letter opener, and the ice turned to the atrium tile, which she had now damaged even worse. The fault line had splintered into branching cracks.

Isla dropped the letter opener, cold with the sensation of eyes on her. With every cell in her body, she prayed that there was no one watching, that the eyes were only in her nightmares.

She looked up and found the mezzanine empty. Her relief had such weight that it made her set her hands on the floor.

But then two eyes gleamed down at her.

Not from the mezzanine.

From the stairs.

The shape of Paz was subtle but jarring, like the shadow of a spider crossing Isla's skin. Paz leaned against the banister, halfway down to the foyer. Instead of a white nightgown, she wore loose-fitting pants and what looked like a men's smoking jacket. The lapels shifted blue as she inhaled and then green as she exhaled, the angle changing the fabric.

Paz laughed without smiling.

Slowly, she opened her hands.

Gold threads shimmered across her fingers.

Her laugh built behind her closed mouth, first lifting the corners and then parting her lips.

The shimmer looked thick and wet, as though Paz had pricked her fingertips and bled molten gold.

Her laugh bloomed, and it echoed off the tile and wood and wallpaper. It caught in the chandelier and ricocheted off every cut gem.

Isla waited for the echoing noise to wake everyone. She wanted it to. A minute ago, she'd wanted no one at the railing. Now she wanted all of them to see the madness in this girl, and to tell her if this was the same madness that had driven them onto the roof, and to tell her if *that* was the same madness that had lit inside Renata like the blue of a gas flame.

But no doors opened. No one appeared. They were all sleeping, or dancing on the roof, or running out toward the blue hills, throwing off their clothes and their manners. They were anywhere and doing anything except coming to witness the impossible blood on Paz's hands.

The gold thickened and spread. And Paz was throwing her head back, thrilled and wild as a flame catching.

TWENTY-THREE

"NOW." EDUARDA PLACED her hands together, the embroidery on her gloves whispering. "I need a volunteer to be my gentleman. Who's feeling gentlemanly?"

No one volunteered. Not even Paz, who was staring into space. She had a haunted expression, and her arms were folded, fists closed, so Isla couldn't look for gold on her hands.

Isla had been trying to talk to her all morning. But she hadn't been at breakfast, and in the halls, she had responded neither to Isla nor to anyone else. When Isla had touched her sleeve, Paz had simply brushed past her.

Eduarda was still waiting for her usual volunteer. Paz was one of the few who ever volunteered to be a gentleman, and the only one who did so consistently. It seemed to be the unspoken reason she was allowed to wear pants as often as she wanted.

Eduarda cleared her throat pointedly.

Paz startled back to attention. She sat up and raised her hand, only from the elbow.

"Yes, Paz, thank you." Eduarda waited for Paz to take her place at the front the room. "And I'll assume the mannish stride is simply because you're getting into character," Eduarda said with forced brightness. "Now, who shall be my lady?"

Paz couldn't avoid Isla in waltz position.

Isla raised her hand.

"Isla." Eduarda practically breathed out her happy surprise, as though this was the sign that Isla had taken her *this is your second chance, young lady* to heart. "Yes, thank you."

Paz had shored up her expression. Her face now told nothing. Her stance was graceful but easy, tall but not rigid. She had fastened her hair low, a cola de caballo at the nape of her neck.

"Stand a little to the right of your gentleman." Eduarda instructed Isla with her hands and her words. "So he can pull you into his arm, not his chest, and so you may both turn your heads without colliding. Gentleman, place your hand."

Paz rested a hand on the back of Isla's rib cage.

"The gentleman's hand goes no farther down than the buttons of your dress," Eduarda said. "If he goes lower, you have my full permission to slap him."

Restrained, good-natured laughter rippled through the lesson room.

I need to talk to you, Isla mouthed more than whispered.

"And my lady, place one hand on your gentleman's shoulder," Eduarda said. "The other in his free hand."

Isla slid her palm onto Paz's shoulder. Hard. "What happened to you last night?" Isla's whisper was veiled by Eduarda's commentary about maintaining an ever-pleasing demeanor.

Paz slipped Isla's hand into hers. The gesture was sure and precise, and she did not respond.

"Head tilted a little to the left," Eduarda said, "only slightly. If you're staring out and away from him, he'll think you find him boring or that you don't trust him not to steer you into another couple."

Isla stared at Paz hard enough that Paz flinched.

"And note how the gentleman guides you," Eduarda said.

With gentle pressure from her hand, Paz drew Isla closer in.

"Remember, he should be directing you," Eduarda said, "not shoving you."

Paz angled Isla so precisely that no one could see Paz set her mouth next to Isla's ear.

"Not here," she said. "Tonight."

TWENTY-FOUR

THE LETTERS FROM HER grandmother were all variations on the same chorus.

A friend of a friend thinks he knows where she might be.

We'll find her.

Don't worry.

Isla could hear the laughter on the roof, the noise fracturing into pieces and then becoming a single sound again. Paz wasn't up there. Isla had checked. She wasn't in her room either. Paz wasn't anywhere in this house, not that Isla could find.

Isla paced the halls, listening for the sound of footsteps or a door opening.

The hallway had mirrors on both sides, so every time she

or anyone else walked down it, it seemed haunted with end-less reflected versions of themselves. But right now, every one of them made Isla turn, looking for Paz.

Paz would talk to her if Isla had to climb into a chande-lier after her. Paz would not follow the Alarie way, the stifling quiet, not about this. Isla would not let her.

Paz had been laughing on the stairs, gold spreading over her hands, a universe apart from the fury in Renata's face as she wielded the letter opener. But there was something in their faces that had almost matched, a sudden, unhinged turn. They looked like something was breaking open in them.

Isla didn't realize what her fingers were doing until her nails scratched the flocked wallpaper. She'd been fidgeting with a stone that had come a little loose from its setting.

A blur of motion drew Isla's eyes to the mirror in front of her.

The motion in the corner of the mirror didn't match the black of Isla's hair, or the brown of her skin, or the blue of her nightgown. The figure in the mirror was so pale her skin seemed translucent. Her hair was a blond so luminous it looked spun from gold. Her dress was a swirling gown of poured copper and platinum.

Abuela had told Isla about holography, and about the Hungarian scientist who had worked with the ghostly green of mercury lamps, figuring out how to diffract a light field into something like a magician's illusion. It was half of how Isla's grandmother had made her fortune. She'd believed in it first. She'd invested in the work of incorporating it into micro-scopes. Science that looked like sorcery, Abuela called it.

This was what this diamond-skinned, gold-haired girl looked like. She looked like a hologram etching embedded in the mirror.

And yet, the fluid way she was moving, the way her thou-sand replicas moved with her, didn't match the jumping dif-fraction of a hologram.

This illusion of a girl and her countless identical sisters were slowly coming up behind Isla.

With movements so small she hoped they were invis-ible, Isla's fingers kept working at the stone. One point of the double-ended cut had already come free, and her fingers moved the jewel back and forth like a loose tooth.

As her hand worked, Isla took one small glance at the hologram of the girl.

Both of their thousand replicas bounced between the two mirrors.

Questions filled Isla's mouth, bitter as ash.

Who are you?

Are you driving these girls mad?

Did you do the same to my sister?

Are you trying to do the same to me?

As though she could hear the unspoken questions, the apparition of the girl and her copies floated forward. Her placement in the mirror meant she was right behind Isla now.

Isla held on to the stone in the wall, caught between

wanting to turn and look and wanting to stop herself. There was no comforting outcome. If the girl was really there, her thousand copies might be too. If she wasn't, Isla's nightmares were following her even when she was awake.

Then the girl smiled.

As her mouth opened wider, her parting lips revealed the dark, tongueless cavern of her throat. She did not have the clear, sparkling teeth of the girl in the chandelier. Her teeth were just as faceted and glittering and pointed, but instead they were red, like garnets or blood-soaked diamonds.

As her smile broadened, her face split into facets. She was breaking apart. The smile she was forcing her mouth into was fracturing her own face. But she was still opening her mouth wider, broadening that sweet, sickening expression. She bared her bloodred teeth, drawing close enough that she disappeared behind Isla.

The moment Isla could feel the chill of the holographic girl's breath on her neck, she knew. The girl wasn't merely etched inside the glass. The girl was as outside the mirror as Isla, and her breath carried the damp cold of a February night.

Isla's blood flickered to life. She pried the jewel the rest of the way out of the wall, warping the gold prongs of the setting. The stone was clear and rich but paler than sapphire. It was a shallow sea, a piece chipped out of the sky. And it was marquise cut, dagger-pointed at both ends.

She whirled around and shoved the knife of the jewel

into the space behind her. The stone threw blue light onto the girl's shirt as Isla held one pointed end to her throat.

It wasn't until the knife of the blue jewel was pressing into the girl's skin that Isla registered the discrepancies.

This was not the diamond-skinned girl with the spun-gold hair and the poured-gold dress.

This was brown skin and true black hair.

This was a white shirt and dark trousers.

In the same moment Isla truly registered who she was trying to stab, she saw the blood on Paz's collar.

Isla had just stabbed Paz.

TWENTY-FIVE

THE JEWEL FELL FROM Isla's fingers.

The stain on Paz's white shirt was proof that she had blood in her veins, and not the molten gold that had been on her hands.

Isla had stabbed her in the neck, yet Paz was still blinking in confusion, as though she didn't quite understand what had happened to her own body.

"Paz," Isla breathed out.

Paz looked down at her shirt.

And she laughed.

Her laugh was not the same laugh as when she had gold on her hands. This one was softer.

"You didn't do anything." She made a show of brushing

her fingers over her shoulders like dusting away lint. "No harm done."

With every word, with every contraction of the muscles in Paz's throat, Isla waited for more blood to pour from her neck.

Isla turned to run for help.

Just as she shifted her weight, Paz grabbed her arm.

"Isla." Paz turned the name into a word so clipped it sounded like one syllable.

Her grip was hard enough to get Isla's attention. It was stronger than Isla would have expected of an injured girl. The shock was keeping her going. Any second blood would pour out of her, and she'd drop.

As she stepped forward, the hall's dim light showed slashes of red.

Paz's face, neck, and shirt were streaked with blood.

Not the fresh red of a new wound.

The brick red of recently dried blood. With her stained, pin-tucked shirt, Paz looked like a romantic poet who'd just murdered a lover.

Paz tracked Isla's eyes as they skipped from one red comet trail to the next.

Her expression changed, the knife-shine of her arrogance coming back.

"I'd like to think we're friends," she said. "So may I offer you a bit of friendly advice?"

Isla couldn't have nodded if she wanted to. The tendons in her neck felt hard as the tines of a fork.

Not because she was afraid of Paz.

She wasn't.

She should have been.

She wasn't.

"Say nothing," Paz told her. "Because you have nothing to say."

A metallic smell bridged the dim space between them. It mixed with the sharp note of Paz's perfume, that scent of white azaleas.

Isla could feel the tang of iron and salt between her teeth. She could feel the thrill of something lighting up inside her, something new and bloodthirsty. She could feel the heat of the blood on Paz's shirt as though it was on her own clothes.

She could feel the thrill of a letter opener in her hand as though her hand belonged to her sister.

"How could you have?" Paz asked. "Because whatever you think I've done, no Alarie girl would ever do it. So how could it have even happened? How could I have ever done it?"

TWENTY-SIX

PAZ WAS BRAZEN.

And the next night, it made her easy to follow.

She wore a white shirt out into the dark. Her black trousers blended in with the night, but because of that shirt, she was as obvious as a moon falling to Earth.

Paz didn't look back. She strode forward into the dark, either believing the Alarie sisters wouldn't follow her or not caring if they did.

Beyond school grounds, the houses were so far apart Isla could barely tell the difference between lit windows and low stars. She picked up the layers of her dress so she could walk without tripping. She wasn't exactly blending in either, thanks to a wardrobe meant to let her blend in at the Alarie

House. The best she'd been able to do was this pale green velvet. The moon drew the silver out of it, and the reflection off the white underskirt almost let her see where she was stepping. If Eduarda decided to take a sweep of the landscape, Isla was finished.

But she had to find out where Paz was going, and why.

The shining examples of the Alarie House were odd, placid, wavering between compliant and erratic. But they seemed to be sleepwalking through it. Paz was the only one Isla had seen with that look of being consumed by something, that look Isla had seen on Renata. Whatever had happened to Renata here, it was happening to Paz.

And if Isla didn't figure out why, it would draw her in next. She could still feel the echo of last night, the flash of madness when she had wanted to be that vicious, that dangerous.

That thrill had kept away the questions that flooded in now, whose blood it was, whether it had come from someone Paz had fought or someone Paz had killed, whether Paz had shut down a fight or gone looking for one.

The leaves on the trees turned spindly. The land grew paler, running toward the hills. Isla tracked Paz's shape against the dark. She copied her path over the rocky ground and alongside the reed-fringed creek beds.

Then Paz disappeared into the darkness. Isla hadn't lost track of her. Paz had just vanished. She opened a door into the dark itself and stepped through into a slash of brilliant daylight.

Paz had torn open the night and slipped forward into sunrise.

Isla ran in the direction of the now-invisible seam. If she got close enough to the horizon, maybe she would find it. She might bump up against it, like running into a curtain.

Then the seam in the universe opened again. That slash of blazing light reappeared.

And Paz stood within it. The sky buckled and waved around her like water as she called out, "Are you coming or not?"

TWENTY-SEVEN

PAZ PUSHED OPEN THE night, throwing aside a panel of blue-violet sky. The panel's movement distorted the silhouetted trees and scattered the stars.

Mirrored glass. The whole structure in front of Isla was mirrored glass. It wasn't a seam in the fabric of the universe; it was a house.

The mirrored walls reflected the blue hills, the purple night, the flashes of pewter beneath the clouds, so the house itself was almost invisible. The only way in was as secret as a trapdoor in a diamond.

And Paz was inviting her inside.

Isla should have been afraid of her.

She wasn't.

She felt it again, that viciousness, and it had enough weight that she could feel it like a blade in her hand. If she needed to, she could rip Paz open with her teeth. She could look pretty while doing it. She could smile sweetly after.

Isla went in.

The sheen of the exterior contrasted with the dust-grayed walls and worn wood tables inside. Everywhere, there were sharp objects, metal tools polished and shining or dulled from time and rust.

There were so many pointed edges. Any one of them could have been the one Paz drove into someone else, spraying their blood onto her own clothes. How cleanly each could have been used to kill. And from the look of them, half of them had been. Splashes of dried red splattered the silver.

If Isla needed to, she could grab that one. Or that one. She could have them at Paz's throat faster than Paz could pull her into waltz position.

"Ingenious, isn't it?" Paz asked. "Anyone looking for it would run right into it. It gives anyone inside a good, loud, rattling alert to unexpected visitors. Or at least it would if anyone ever came out here."

There were so many jewelers' loupes it looked like a lab. There were simple ones with a single lens, new ones with achromatic lenses, sets attached to glasses. A miniature loupe with a sliding brass cover was so small Isla could have hidden it in her brassiere.

The glass reservoir under one lens held a stone so red it looked like a drop of blood.

The smell of iron clotted in Isla's throat. Her eyes found a jar of bloodred.

"Ferric oxide," Paz said as she cleaned one of the glass loupes. "Otherwise known as jeweler's rouge. It makes the most wonderful polish."

The image of Paz in a bloodstained shirt transformed into her concentrating over a lapidary wheel.

Cut and uncut stones glinted on tables and in vises. Partly faceted jewels looked like statues emerging from marble. Marking pens and precision tools were slashed with not just the red of jeweler's rouge but with green wax.

This was the wood and metal clutter that belonged to a lapidary.

"You stand in what was once a much-storied workshop." Paz stood in the center of the space. "Once upon a time, every jewel that ended up in the Alarie House walls was cut here."

TWENTY-EIGHT

ISLA'S BRAIN TURNED THE sharp objects from deadly knives to lapidary's tools, the red from blood to polishing rouge.

"Long before our time." Paz strolled from one table to the next. "Before some falling out between the gem cutters and the Alaries.

"What happened?" Isla asked.

"I don't know. Probably something about someone wearing the wrong hat for the wrong season." Paz examined raw stones as though checking the progress of repotted plants. "I don't blame them for leaving. How long could anyone really put up with that family telling you what to do all the time?"

The blood-soaked spell was gone, and now Isla was waking up to what they were both doing.

"Do the Alarie sisters know you're here?" Isla asked.

Paz's laugh rang through the air. "Yes, that's exactly why I slip away under cover of night and then back in before sunrise. Because they bless all this. They couldn't be happier for me."

"Aren't you afraid of getting caught?" Isla asked.

Paz held up a gem to a lit candle. "They don't do anything after lights-out." She held the same stone up to lamplight, and the color shifted. "They don't consider any of it their problem."

Isla called up Carina's warnings. "Girls have gotten thrown out for being caught with boys. Or other girls."

"Oh, that?" Paz held the stone up to the cold glow of a work lamp, and veins of purple showed. "You really have to shove it in their faces for them to do something. And the last time it happened, the girl did, so they had to kick her out. I think she wanted to get expelled. She was sneaking her boyfriend in, and he was one of the more distinguished underage drunks in his very distinguished family. Enough that he almost came in the wrong window. So they didn't really have a choice. If you don't make them look right at something though, they won't."

Paz brought a teal stone up to a candle, and it went flame orange. "This is, of course, a profession utterly unsuitable to a proper young lady. So they'd really rather not know I'm studying for it. Therefore, they don't know."

Isla kept a steady distance between her and Paz. When

Paz came forward, she moved back. But now, as Paz went to the farther tables, Isla took cautious steps forward. "Where did you learn to do this?"

"My aunt is a lapidarist." By moving from one lamp to another, Paz turned a burgundy jewel green. "Much to the agony of my family, of course, for what lady would engage in such a violent and messy profession?" Paz gestured to the sharp edges of the tools, the stains of what still looked so much like blood even though Isla now knew better.

"She taught me as much as she could without my parents knowing, but it was getting more and more difficult to hide it," Paz said. "So when my parents proposed a finishing school, she suggested one of the most prestigious in the world. Which, she knew, just happened to have an abandoned lapidary workshop that she suggested I use to practice what she's taught me."

Isla watched Paz turn a yellow gem to pink with a flick of her wrist, one light source to another.

"She started me off cleaning dops, sharpening tools, then practicing with glass replicas." Paz held another stone under a lamp, and it lit up like phosphorescent paint. "It was how I learned. I still use glass to try out different cuts."

Paz held up a mineral rough striped with purple, green, and blue. "This one's giving me quite the challenge because of how shallow it is." She tapped a nearby notebook opened to a double spread of unlined paper. Paz had sketched a dozen faceted shapes from different angles. "The more you want something to catch the light"—she turned the rough, showing a vein of indigo—"the less of it you end up with."

Isla could feel the blank look taking over her face. She wasn't following, and it was the same feeling, a sense of trying to catch up to something, that she had while watching the older Alarie girls.

Paz set two diamonds on the table. "A rose cut." She pointed to one. "A brilliant cut." She pointed to the other. "Both stones started out the same weight."

The rose cut was a demure point of light, but the brilliant looked as though it had about a thousand more facets. When the light from the lamp hit it, it glittered like fine snow.

"The brilliant sparkles more, but because you've cut more facets into it, you've lost more of its original weight," Paz said. "Whenever you shape something, whenever you polish something, you lose part of it. It's an inherent feature of the art form." Paz polished a viewing glass with a cloth. "But don't let diamonds overly impress you. Diamonds may be hard. But they're brittle. They break easily. There are better things to be than a diamond."

"Like a sapphire?" Isla pointed to Paz's throat, between the panels of her shirt collar. The blue stone was smooth and rounded rather than faceted, and its setting was suspended from a thin black cord. It cast deep, watery blue into the shadowing between Paz's breasts. "Odd choice for you, isn't it?"

"Oh?" Paz asked. "Why's that?"

"My abuela told me they were historically considered sacred," Isla said. "Emblematic of heaven. Encouraging of pure thoughts."

"I don't care much for pure thoughts." Paz lifted it away from her throat. "Or pure stones."

She turned the sapphire so it caught the light from a different angle. "See the fibrous inclusions?" They looked like white rays reaching out through the stone. "They form when little wisps of titanium dioxide are caught in the mineral as it forms. It's how you get a silk stone. When the silk gathers along three axes, then it's a star stone. Asterism. Helen of Troy had a star sapphire, and according to legend, it was the source of her power, her hold over men. Star stones have long had a reputation for being powerful charms. All because of something that's technically a flaw."

The light stretched the filaments of silk to the edges of the sapphire. The white grew sharper, and the blue turned brighter and clearer, like the sky before sunrise.

"But it's a flaw you can never cut away," Paz said. "You'll never get rid of it no matter how much you try."

It sounded like a threat, enough that the vicious rush came back into Isla. She could be just like Renata if she wanted. Beautiful and frightening. So beautiful and so frightening that people could only look at her in glances, and only come near her if she let them.

"With diamonds you can plan around the carbon spots, the pinpoints, the needles and feathers," Paz said. "You cut away as many as you can away from the heart of the stone. But with star stones, that flaw is the heart. Even if you smash the stone into smithereens, each piece contains the whole star."

Paz took a step closer to Isla.

Isla did not move back.

She took the sapphire between her fingers. She wanted Paz to think she had it in her to tear it from her throat.

"Want to put it on your tongue?" Paz asked.

Isla pinched the stone tighter to keep the flinch off her face.

Paz smiled. "They're conductive. They draw heat from your body. If you put a ruby or a sapphire in your mouth, it feels like ice."

Paz was looking at her so intently, and Isla realized she was waiting for Paz to say Renata's name. There was no Isla without Renata. That was the essence of Isla, a small copy of Renata, lesser in both body and heart.

She was Renata's little sister before she was herself, and she kept waiting for the comparison.

You don't look much like your sister. Or *You look just like your sister.*

You remind me a little of Renata. Or *You two aren't much alike, are you?*

But Paz didn't say any of this. The quiet between them, that unspoken name, caught Isla off guard enough that she let the sapphire go. It fell back against Paz's skin.

Isla hated how sharply she wanted this. But right now, in

this workshop, she was her own girl. She wasn't just the lesser Soler sister. For a minute, she almost believed it, that she held the enchanting charm of any Alarie girl.

And she wanted to know it for sure, to prove it. She wanted to be the kind of girl who was beautiful enough to get something from someone as beautiful as Paz.

A green uncut stone sat on a nearby table, rough and varied as green ice. It was deep, vivid, translucent. A raw emerald.

Isla held it up. "Can I have it?"

Paz smiled, a soft laugh behind her lips. "Only if you let me show you what's inside it."

TWENTY-NINE

PAZ SET THE RAW emerald under a microscope. "Look into the piece there."

Isla bent low enough to look. When she did, she was in a green sea, with rippling green currents and delicate trails of green bubbles.

"You're looking at flaws," Paz said. "Inclusions. They're technically considered blemishes, but they're the magic in the stone."

Even through her dress, Isla could feel the heat of Paz's body.

"Do you see how wet it looks?" Paz asked. "Emeralds don't sparkle. They shine like that, like they're water."

Paz's scent mixed with the smells in the workshop. It was minerals, wax and iron, and the smoke and earth of evergreen branches, as though Paz had slipped through the trees to sneak out here.

"This is what people forget," Paz said. "Diamonds are made rare by the machinations of men. They create the illusion of scarcity, when most gems, diamonds included, occur all over this planet, in all different places, in many colors. But emeralds can only be the result of the most improbable and reckless collision of tectonic plates. The elements in emeralds don't occur in similar terrains. So without that great collision, without sufficient force and pressure and serendipity, they don't form."

The green looked alive. Isla half expected silvery fish to swim through.

"This is what I love most about emeralds," Paz said. "How unlikely they are to even exist in the first place."

Paz slipped one palm onto Isla's back.

Isla stayed looking into the microscope, that sea of green. She stayed in Paz's hold.

She let Paz take one of her hands.

Paz was close but didn't put her body against Isla's. Her carriage was confident but distant. It would have seemed like practice for waltz position if Paz wasn't behind her.

Isla stared deeper into that world of luminous green.

"The color you're looking at," Paz said, "that's from chromium, a trace impurity. An imperfection. The more of that imperfection you have, the greener the stone."

The pressure of Paz's hand was so precise that Isla moved closer to her before she even realized she was doing it.

"Emeralds make their own light," Paz said, "all because of that imperfection. The introduction of something different creates the most unimaginable splendor. Imperfection makes things glow."

Isla could see the shadows of her own eyelashes against the green.

"Even jewelers," Paz said, "the very eyes searching for flaws, revere the flaws within the emerald. They even have a name for them. Le jardin. A garden held within a jewel."

The layers of Isla's skirt whispered against Paz's trousers.

"That's what it takes, fire and water and heat." Paz's words were feathers against Isla's neck. "And two things that almost never come together."

A thread of lightning stirred in Isla.

Isla turned around, like a half spin in a dance.

Paz backed her against the worktable, and the velvet of her skirt gathered against the edge.

Isla lifted the sapphire from Paz's collarbone and put it in her mouth. The jewel chilled her tongue. The cord was a dark whisper on her lips, and the sapphire tasted like salt and lemon.

With her eyes still on Paz, Isla took the sapphire from her mouth as delicately as a hard candy. "You're right. It's cold."

She set it back against Paz's skin, the jewel still wet from her mouth. She could feel the thread of lightning against Paz's shirt and her dress. The smell of white azaleas drifted off the fabric and mixed with the flat smell of wax and the sharpness of metal.

Paz kissed her, and the taste on Paz's tongue matched the taste of the sapphire, lemon-bitter and deep blue.

They were elements from completely different parts of the planet. They were ocean floor and mountain caves. They were crashing into each other with enough force to make emeralds.

THIRTY

"**AND SO YOU SEE,**" Eduarda said, "you can work wonders with milk of roses, olive oil, and simple flower water."

Each girl sat at a small wood table fixed with a round mirror. Bottles filled with different oils and waters wafted their mild scents through the air.

"Where were you last night?" Carina asked when Eduarda was distracted at the opposite corner of the room.

"The Provençal variation uses rosemary." Eduarda smiled as though revealing a secret. "The Alsatians employ almonds and lavender."

Carina reached for a fluted glass jar. "Laureana snuck us into town."

"And with rosewater and the right oils, you have your very own homemade cold cream," Eduarda said.

"She even got us a suite at the hotel, though she wouldn't say how." Carina made a show of examining the rosewater, presumably in case Eduarda looked over. "Someone half in love with her."

"Honey water and distilled wine can do wonders for the hair," Eduarda said, "but take down the measurements very carefully, ladies. Goodness help you if you mix it incorrectly. You'll have a mess on your hands."

Paz caught Isla's eye in the mirror. Isla looked away, but the heat of Paz watching her radiated through her back.

"And remember"—Eduarda did a flourish with her hands as though conducting an orchestra—"good grooming begins before you even wash your face in the morning. It begins with beauty sleep. And a few favorite petals to perfume your linen never did a girl any harm."

Carina leaned toward Isla on the pretense of borrowing extra rose petals. "Come join us tonight."

Isla glanced toward Eduarda. "What about beauty sleep?"

"No girl is pretty when she's dour, no matter how well rested," Carina said. "We all need our fun, don't we?"

"Lavender, rose, bergamot, these are lovely things to put in your Florence oil for your hair," Eduarda said. "But not too much, as too much of anything can disturb the natural health of the scalp. All things in moderation, ladies."

"Even moderation." Carina elbowed Isla.

Carina was so drunk with this place that the older girls could have convinced her to walk to the horizon and bring back the setting moon. She wanted everything here so badly that the sparkle of the jewels intoxicated her.

And you don't?

That whisper, the echo of Renata's voice, drifted from the walls. Isla looked around, knowing Renata wouldn't be there, her reflex to look for her still taking over.

Carina hadn't heard. She was crushing rose petals between her fingers. Neither had anyone else. They were following the lesson, measuring out drops of oil.

You're one of them, hermanita, came the whisper from the walls. The last word pinched the center of Isla's heart. *You're one of us. You'd realize if you only stopped to see it.*

"You're considering it," Carina whispered. "I can tell. I promise you'll have a good time."

Renata and Paz had nothing in common except that they had both been enrolled here at the same time. Paz's charm had an antagonistic edge, daring anyone to say anything about her pants or her posture. Whatever Paz did, she wanted you to know. The point was you knowing. The act of disruption was as much an accessory as her cuff links.

Paz didn't want any of this. It was a formality, something to appease her family.

But there was something here for Isla. Renata had believed it with such fierce conviction that it had carved her whispers into the walls of this place.

Isla could do this, learning manners from the Alarie sisters and gestures from the Alarie girls. She could learn to do them as well as any girl who'd been born with all the pieces her body was supposed to have and none of the pieces it wasn't. In fact, she'd learn them better. The thousand small things that made up the art of being an Alarie girl mattered even more with Isla. They were the thing that would cover her more than the padding in her brassiere or the layers of her skirts. The Alarie House magic was like clouds of meringue icing, so thick that no one could tell what kind of cake was underneath.

Renata was beckoning her from the other side of a door. Isla just needed enough nerve to walk through.

"Foyer. At midnight. Just like Cinderella." Carina gave a conspiring smile. "If her shoes were made of diamonds instead of glass."

THIRTY-ONE

AT LEAST A DOZEN girls clustered along the mezzanine railing. They were all in their nightgowns, layered and immaculate as spring tea dresses, but they were barefoot. One by one, a few of them were climbing into the enormous chandelier. Their hands gripped the brass arms. They walked on the garlands of diamonds that made up the lower basket of the chandelier. If they felt the sharp edges of the jewels against the soles of their feet, their faces didn't show it.

They were a whirl of pastel nightgowns, shining hair, fingernails flashing like rose quartz. More arrived in the halls, until half the house must have been there. The blonde whose round blue eyes always looked startled, especially when Eduarda excitedly clapped her hands. The girl with dark skin who wore a different shade of pastel mauve every day, and who was always trying to read a book under the table at breakfast. The sisters who were perpetually taking up the entire mirror in the bathroom, blocking all access to the sink until they were done reviewing the latest gossip from their hometown.

They looked like Muses posing on enchanted swings, or mermaids in dazzling nets. The distance to the foyer seemed lost on them. They held the jeweled cords as though they were the ropes of a swing. They swayed the chandelier back and forth, their laughter in perfect rhythm with its chime and rattle. They showed no fear. The rush of the height seemed as intoxicating to them as champagne.

"I've heard no one was better at this than your sister," Carina said. "Rumor is she could do it without even rattling the jewels."

Isla could almost believe it. She could almost connect the Alarie House version of Renata with the sister she knew. There was an artistry to Renata's recklessness. It wasn't that she wanted to scandalize anyone; it was more that she didn't care if she did. Renata thought nothing of crossing the richest daughters in town, no matter how vindictive they might be (Renata had more than once been banned from the best dress shops). When she was volunteering at the church, she treated communion wafers like snack food; at the horrified faces of any onlookers, she said, *What? These ones aren't consecrated. It's not Jesus until it's consecrated.*

To Renata, climbing into those jewels, looking absolutely

splendid while she did it, would have been a siren's song of a challenge.

The girls reached their fingers through the chandelier. They didn't avoid looking down. They made a point to. They gazed at the floor as though it was fogged-over glass, or a frozen pond, or a sheet of diamond refracting everything, so that all they could get was a vague, dull impression of what was on the other side.

As the chandelier spun in slow circles, graceful arms extended toward the floor. The chandelier looked like it was growing beautiful, ladylike tentacles.

They were all awake. But maybe they, too, were sharing in the nightmare that had grabbed hold of Isla. Maybe they, too, saw something under the floor. A clot of red—was it blood or strawberry jam?—under a shell of ice. A garnet beneath a sheet of diamond. Their own hearts held within leaded glass.

When another girl climbed into the jeweled net, a space opened. Carina moved along the railing, closer to the chandelier. She looked mesmerized, like a kitten batting at a flicker of light on a wall.

She put a knee up on the wrought iron and began to transfer her weight.

The second she did, the distance to the foyer floor yawned open.

Isla reached out. "Carina, no." She grabbed her arm.

Carina gripped the railing so hard her knuckles paled. She looked right at Isla, and she screamed. She screamed so loudly Isla thought a window would shatter, and when the other girls joined in, Isla thought the whole chandelier would disintegrate into sparkling confetti.

As they screamed together, their edges seemed to grow sharper, as though they were turning to cut minerals. Carina's features looked refracted through rippling water or broken glass. Her mouth, all of their mouths, were not mouths but cracks in the earth. The teeth were not teeth but jagged, glittering fields of crystals. Light came from the backs of their throats, but not the champagne-soft light from the chandelier. It was hot and dim, like their hearts were not hearts but the molten core of the earth.

The longer they screamed, the more Isla was sure that they were going to break themselves apart right along with the chandelier. They would turn to shimmering pieces flying everywhere. They would be nothing but beautiful, broken smithereens.

It wasn't just Renata.

It had never just been Renata.

Renata's madness was a thing shared between so many Alarie girls.

Isla let Carina go.

The screaming stopped.

No one smiled at Isla.

No one glared at her.

No one gave her the sympathetic look they'd given her on

the roof. None of them gave her any look at all. The moment she released her grip, they all went on as they'd been before.

Even Carina turned away from Isla. Not as though making a point. More like she had forgotten Isla was there the instant Isla let go.

The echo of the screaming hung in the air. It was that high-pitched ringing, that sound like a finger circling a half-filled wine flute.

Dread flared through Isla, fast as a drop of color through hot water. Maybe they'd all gotten away with the screaming on the roof, but this was different. This was inside. This was right under where the Alarie sisters slept.

"Carina, we have to go," Isla said. They might still be able to make it back to their rooms.

If the Alarie sisters threw Isla out, Isla would lose the one thread she had connecting her to Renata. She could feel it in the air here, something invisible that her hands kept clutching at.

"Carina," Isla said.

Carina wanted to be here more than she wanted any frilled dress, any perfume bottle, any jewelry in the world. Carina didn't want to get thrown out of here any more than Isla did.

But she wasn't moving. Carina held tight to the railing, staring at the tiers of jewels as though watching a queen.

Any second the Alarie sisters were going to rush down

the stairs. Isla knew nothing about the proper, ladylike way to rip a bunch of girls' heads off, but they were all about to be part of a live demonstration.

Except the Alarie sisters did not appear.

Girls languorously spun in the chandelier, and the stairwell from the third floor stayed quiet.

Paz had been right. The Alarie sisters didn't even seem to be able to hear them.

But where was Paz? She wasn't in the chandelier. She wasn't along the railing with the other girls reaching their hands out for the crystals, waiting for their turn to climb in. She wasn't even looking on, laughing with molten metal on her hands.

That was when Isla saw it, the bead of liquid gold falling past the window, like a drop of gilded rain.

THIRTY-TWO

AS SOON AS ISLA climbed out the window and onto the eave, she saw it all. Gold dripped off the edges of the tiles like honey. It flecked the trees like snow. The bougainvillea and morning glories looked dipped in gilt paint.

And there, on the highest slope of the roof, stood Paz, her polished boots streaked with it. She tilted her face to the sky, breathing in the wind. She held herself with the same proprietary air she'd had in the lapidary workshop.

Her eyes were closed, her expression absorbed as if she was listening to an orchestra. But there was nothing out here except the sound of the trees whispering. So she was either listening to them, or to the distant sounds of the chandelier inside the house. It chimed underneath them as girls climbed in and out.

"There's an old story about Elizabeth I." Paz opened her eyes but didn't look at Isla. "Likely apocryphal. I don't really believe anything that anyone tries to tell me about a royal colonizadora."

There was a humming in the air, a high, piercing noise like the ring around the other girls' screams.

Paz kept looking up. "For all her kingdom, for everything at her fingertips, she lusted after something she could not have," Paz said. "An enormous teardrop pearl Philip of Spain had given Mary Tudor."

Isla took a step closer, the roof slick with gold under her bare feet.

Paz did not look at her. She stared up at the night sky like the stars were raw diamonds she'd been tasked with cutting. "It was the largest pearl ever known at that time, and Elizabeth wanted it. Badly. But Mary didn't want her to have it. She made sure that when she died it would be returned to Philip in Spain."

Paz took a step to the side, as though pondering a star from another angle, imagining a different shaping. "So Elizabeth instituted a generous policy toward the piracy of Spanish ships. On one condition. Said pirates had to pledge to bring her the pearl should they find it."

The wind blew Paz's hair around her, one lock a dark slash across her throat.

"She never did get it," Paz said. "But she took down a lot of ships trying. Any guesses as to the moral of this story?"

Isla took another step forward. Her foot hit a slick of gold. She lost her balance and started to slide.

Paz's arm flew out. Her hand grabbed Isla's forearm hard enough that it steadied her.

No fear showed on Paz's face.

"The moral," she said, "is that spite can do immensely powerful things."

The roof tiles seemed as though they were buckling, rippling like water.

"Paz," Isla said. "What's happening in this house?"

Paz anchored her fingers into Isla's arm, and she smiled. "Whatever I want."

THIRTY-THREE

FINGERS OF COLD AIR wrapped around Isla's throat.

"Las hermanas, they're not paying attention."

The force of Paz's hold was keeping Isla up, stopping her from falling toward the edge. "So I do whatever I want."

The fingers of Paz's free hand went to her neck, to that sapphire. It seemed like an involuntary gesture, something protective.

Paz's stories flickered through Isla's brain like the filaments of white silk in that blue stone.

Helen of Troy. Her star sapphire. The source of her power. Paz had been telling Isla the truth this whole time.

Isla just hadn't listened.

The strangeness haunting the Alarie House was thanks to Paz.

"Why?" Isla asked.

"Because I despise this place," Paz said. "Because this place tells me what kind of woman I'm supposed to be, and it's the kind of woman that leaves no room for what I actually am."

Spite. Anger. Rage. Isla could hear it all twisted together in Paz's voice. And how could Isla blame Paz for any of it? The only choice Paz had had was which finishing school, not whether she would go in the first place. In order to be allowed to wear pants here, Paz had had to ingratiate, serve, connive.

"Are you really going to tell me it leaves room for you?" Paz asked.

Now Isla had her own spite, her own anger, her own rage, all of it directed at Paz. Isla was like all the other girls here. Or she could be. And she wanted to prove it. She wanted to rip out her own heart and show it to Paz as a perfectly faceted ruby.

"Places like this set the standard for everyone else," Paz said.

Isla was losing where she was in space. The slicked roof was going out from under them.

"Do you know how they do it?" Paz asked.

They were sliding, Isla on her bare feet, Paz on the polished soles of her boots.

"They choose a few girls we all get to be measured against,"

Paz said. "A few girls become the example the whole world gets to judge us by."

Isla scrambled, trying to get her footing back.

"Speaking of which"—Paz held on to Isla harder—"how's your sister these days?"

Isla's rage caught, quick as a flame on a stove.

Paz hadn't just done this to Isla, to Carina, to all the girls in the house now.

She'd done this to Renata.

And that smile said she wanted Isla to know it.

There was no regret, no remorse.

Only spite.

THIRTY-FOUR

ISLA'S RAGE WAS GOING to spark from her fingertips. It was going to set fire to the drapes in the house. It was going to short out every lamp.

Paz was the vengeful spirit here, like a phantom growing within quartz. The Alarie sisters may have presided over everything from skirt length to how far from the table everyone placed their chairs. But what haunted this place, what had haunted Renata, was because of Paz. It *was* Paz.

The girls in this house weren't just going mad.

Paz was driving them to it.

Isla's anger closed in, like flames licking at the edges of paper. Heat roiled across her shoulders.

When it broke, it smashed through everything holding it back.

And it made her as hard as diamonds.

Isla shoved Paz. Fast as light glancing off an opal, she had Paz on her back. She was kneeling on her, pinning her down.

"What did you do to my sister?" She bit the words between her teeth as she said them.

Paz's tied-back hair came loose and fell over the collar of her shirt.

"Go on," she said. "Do it."

They were so close to the edge that Paz's hair was trailing off, dark ribbons twirling in the air.

"You want to." Paz lifted her chin. "I can tell you want to."

What Isla wanted was to dig her nails into Paz's neck and find out if she had blood in her or just molten gold.

"You want to throw me off this roof," Paz said. "Don't pretend you don't."

"What did you do?" Isla yelled it at her.

Paz gave Isla a taunting smile. "Hours upon days of polite little lessons and meaningless polite conversation, and right now all you want is to follow your worst impulses." She gave a slight glance toward the darkness beyond the roofline. "Who could blame you?" She looked back at Isla, smile still in place even after looking down. "And how precious of a jewel can I really be if I'm afraid of breaking?"

Isla loosened her grip.

She would not let Paz win. She would not let the madness Paz had set loose in this house win.

Isla's gaze caught on the sapphire, the blue dark as a storm.

As Paz breathed, the light refracted into violet. The moon found the pale white needles in the center, the inclusions lighting up into a six-pointed star.

"You know so much about jewels?" Isla asked. "Here's your chance to prove it."

Abuela had taught Isla about the science of light. About holograms. About how some colors were really there and some were illusions.

"There's a difference between the shimmer of an opal and the sparkle of a sapphire," Isla said. "If you can tell me what it is, I might not throw you off this roof."

Paz blinked twice before answering. "Opals are iridescent." Her voice was calm, the tremble underneath it almost imperceptible. "They physically refract light. They change it. Sapphires get their sparkle from the light around them. The excitation of electrons appears blue to the human eye."

"Exactly," Isla whispered.

The velvet glow of that sapphire was a lie made of light. And Paz knew it. As soon as there was no more light, the color and sparkle disappeared.

Girls like Isla and Renata, girls like Carina, they were opals. The lightning and fire they held was something physical and real.

Paz held nothing except the fleeting shimmer of a sapphire. If you took the light away, the blue was gone.

Isla lowered her lips to Paz's collarbone. She took the sapphire in her mouth. It was cold on her tongue, a knot coated in frost. She gripped the cord between her teeth and pulled on it until the fastening knot gave.

Paz flinched, holding a grunt at the back of her throat.

The second the sapphire broke away, Paz looked destroyed, hollowed, as though Isla had just bitten out her heart.

Isla pulled Paz back onto the roof. "You're going to leave now," she said in a perfect finishing school voice. "And you're never going to come near me or my sister or anyone in this house ever again."

THIRTY-FIVE

ISLA STOOD UP THERE, watching.

She wouldn't fall. She knew she wouldn't fall. She
was as invincible as the gold dripping from the white
morning glories.

Isla tied the sapphire around her own throat. Her fingers
knotted the cord at the base of her neck. The chill of the stone
settled into her collarbone.

She stayed up there long enough to watch Paz leave the
house. Paz did not run. She simply walked out into the night,
suitcase at her side.

Isla climbed back through the window, and back into
the house. With each step, she left wet gold footprints on the
deep wood of the floorboards.

The other girls did not notice her at first. When they

did, they looked at her as though she'd appeared from nothing. They regarded her like an unexpected yet welcomed guest. *Oh, where did you come from? Isn't this a surprise?*

But by the time Isla climbed onto the railing, they were all watching.

She did not reach out for the crystal net of the chandelier. She did not scramble into its basket. She walked along the wrought iron railings without holding her arms out for balance. Her bare feet left marks with each step, gilding the dark sheen of the railing.

When she slipped into the chandelier, she did not jump or flail. She did not settle into the jeweled netting. She stood against the central column, holding the brass fixture above her. She did it all so smoothly the crystals did not rattle.

The other girls in the chandelier lounged among the jewels as though they were floating in light, and now, Isla was one of them. She was at the heart of this beautiful creature made of all these Alarie girls in one glittering shell. She occupied the same point in space that Renata had.

Isla knew her sister now, more than ever. If Abuela didn't find her, Isla would. And when they found her, Isla would know her as well as if she were inside her sister's bones. She would know who her sister had become while she was here. The moment she slipped into the chandelier, Isla inhabited her.

Isla was a girl who could be as sweet or as vicious as she needed to be.

She didn't fear the girls around her, not the ones in this house, not the ones years ago at school.

Isla had destroyed the version of herself who lived in that kind of fear. That Isla Soler was gone. She had driven a crystal knife through her heart.

THIRTY-SIX

IN THE MORNING, ISLA saw what they saw, how the weather was so perfect it might as well have been a bolt of fabric in a custom-ordered shade of blue. The sun was bright and thin, the day cooled by ribbons of clouds.

Pretty girls in white dresses and scallop-edged white gloves sat at white tables in the garden. None of them spoke of the night before. None of them needed to. The only conversation was the whispering of the breeze through the leaves, the flat clattering of cups and plates, the shifting of pea gravel under shined heels.

When the Alarie sisters asked if anyone had seen Paz, Isla said she had no idea where she'd gotten to. She said it with appropriate surprise, as though the thought had only just occurred to her. *No, now that you mention it, I haven't seen her.*

But when no one was looking, Isla took Renata's diamond ring off her finger and scratched messages on every window she could get to. The etchings would be beacons to Renata, telling her that Isla had driven out the vengeful ghost of this place, and that it was safe to come back.

Every time Renata had scratched messages into windowpanes, the scraping sound had made Isla wince. But now the screeching of diamond over glass was piercing and perfect as a bird of prey's call.

She's gone. She's gone. She's gone. Isla wrote it over and over, in the scrolling handwriting of a finishing school girl.

THIRTY-SEVEN

AT NIGHT, SHE WALKED the halls with gold still on her feet. It was dim enough that she couldn't see the floor, she could only see where she'd just been, each step gilded in the dark.

A pale blue fog like on winter mornings blew through the halls. It carried in the sound of voices, but not the voices of the other finishing school girls. They were all sleeping, the threshold seams of their doors dark.

The cold carried in voices Isla hadn't heard in years.

Isla banged her hands on every door, trying to wake up Carina, Beth, Gianna, any of them. But they slept on.

She called their names.

They did not stir.

She reached to open the doors, but the knobs vanished

under her fingers. Each one turned to brass vapor as soon as she touched it.

The voices from years ago poured in, the fog thick as smoke. Isla tried to find the stairwell to the third floor. It led to nothing but the star-peppered night. She tried to find the front door, but it was a mirrored panel that only reflected her back into the house. She couldn't even tell where she was stepping anymore. The hem of her nightgown blurred together with the mist around her ankles.

Those voices brought the sound of cutting whispers, the vicious laughter, the name Isla had been called over and over, so many times that she felt it etching into her ribs.

They had known. They all knew there was something wrong with the younger Soler girl.

The boys at school threatened Isla to stay away from their fathers' fields so she wouldn't curse the heifers. They said Isla must have had a brother, because their fathers told them that was the way it always worked with cows whenever there was a cow like Isla. There was always a brother. But no one had ever met her brother, they said, so Isla must have killed him. Her insistence that he never existed was proof that she was not only a murderer, but also a liar.

Girls said Isla couldn't play with them because she wasn't really like them, didn't belong with them. That left her conspicuously alone, crushed beneath the unbearable sympathy of the nicest, most pitying teachers.

Now, tonight, Isla was on her knees, driving the heels of

her hands into the floor, breaking everything she could just so she didn't have to hear those voices. The ground under her was a sheet of faceted quartz, and the only thing she could see underneath it was a twirl of faint light. Down there, her heart was a star ruby, the center milky and illuminated with filaments of silk.

Even her heart was not a normal heart. Nothing about her had been as normal as it was supposed to be. Isla had gotten her hair pulled because they wanted to know if it felt like the switch at the end of a cow's tail. She had gotten held by her wrist because they wanted to find out whose hands her hands looked most like, each reluctant volunteer cringing as though they might draw the short straw.

She was smashing everything she could to block out that laughter and the threat it carried. She pushed back against the feeling that those words were engraving themselves onto her ribs.

She was splintering the floor underneath her to get at her own faceted heart.

Those voices, that laughter, those names, they weren't supposed to be here. Isla wasn't supposed to be afraid of any of them anymore.

The quartz fractured. The ruby shattered into drops of blood. And still that star was there, in every drop, a constellation held in countless red blood cells.

This time, when Isla woke up, she saw herself driving the metal hilt of the hand mirror into the tile. This time, she didn't stop. She didn't drop the mirror. She kept going. She drove it harder into the floor. The crack turned to a gash, a dark trench in the white tile.

Isla broke the painted porcelain until she was sure an aquifer of her own blood wasn't under the floor. She may have been smashing her own heart into pieces, but she would do it if it would shut them all up, if it would stop those names from being scored onto her bones.

THIRTY-EIGHT

THIS TIME, THE ALARIE sisters were going to say something. There was a hole in the foyer. Isla was destroying the house.

Isla almost wanted them to say something. She wanted to know there were limits to what might have happened when Renata was here, that there were things in which the ever-pleasant Alarie sisters would have intervened.

So Isla stood in the foyer, right in front of the gash, daring the Alarie sisters to ask her about it. She looked every bit the part of a finishing school girl. The sun through the windows turned her cream dress to pure light. She could rattle off rules like Alba giving a lesson. *Introduce the younger guest to the elder first. Never ask after a woman's "husband" or "children." They have names; use them. Fingers lightly on the banister; no death grips.*

Luisa stopped in front of her, eyes moving between Isla and the crevice that Isla's raging hands had opened up in the floor.

"Isla, dear," Luisa said, "a lady does not stop at an obstacle and ponder it endlessly. It is both unseemly and unproductive."

Luisa stepped down into the atrium and breezed past the broken tiling.

Her skirts flicked as she ascended the steps on the other side. "She summons her composure and simply goes around it."

THIRTY-NINE

ISLA SAT IN THE space where the fine gravel and flower beds gave way to open land. The grasses were wispy as spun sugar, and they offered two different guards between Isla and everyone else. First, the stalks were tall enough to hide her. Second, what finishing school girl was going to traipse out into knee-high growth?

"Isla?" A distinctive shadow—very short, hair down, skirt puffier than most—fell across the grass. "Is something wrong?"

Isla's plan had apparently underestimated Carina.

"Whatever would be wrong?" Isla said in her best finishing school voice, a combination of Luisa, and Alba, and Eduarda, and then Renata and Carina. And every other girl on the planet who had been born knowing things Isla didn't and being things Isla wasn't.

"I promise I don't mean this in the passive-aggressive way that people say it when they want to insult you and pretend they didn't insult you," Carina said, "but you look tired."

"I'm just having bad dreams," Isla said.

Carina sat down next to Isla, her skirt like pink frosting on the grass. "About what?"

With anyone else, Isla would have said it was none of her business, or something far less polite. But there was something admirable about Carina actually asking. There was no disingenuous *You don't have to tell me if you don't want to*. There was no uncomfortable twist of the upper lip at the mention of an unpleasant topic. Carina was offering to venture away from the manicured lawns of polite conversation and into the wild undergrowth.

So Isla told her, in as few words and in as little detail as possible. Nothing about her body. But enough. Isla told Carina that she didn't like thinking about the last time she was in school, and that was that. Children were smarter and more ruthless than adults gave them credit for, and that was that. There was nothing further to discuss. Isla gave Carina just enough to give her the idea and, at the same time, give her tacit permission to close the topic.

Carina scooted a little closer. "It's awful, isn't it?"

Isla could not have been less in the mood. Carina's

sympathy was going to be a cloying syrup, and politeness would demand Isla pour it directly into her tea and pretend to enjoy it.

But Carina did not look at Isla. She looked only at her own knees. "You don't want to let them get to you, but they do. You don't want to let them see that they're getting to you, but they know. They always know."

Isla looked at Carina, who still looked only at her own skirt.

"You start being afraid of everything," Carina said, "and you feel silly for being afraid of everything because nothing's really wrong except that a few people you can't avoid know exactly what to say that's going to stick to the inside of your brain."

"Does that happen to you here?" Isla asked. Had she been so wrapped up in everything that she hadn't noticed? Was there someone else she needed to threaten on the roof?

Carina shook her head. "A long time ago."

The words hovered, unadorned, in the air.

Isla had thought of Carina as the kind of girl the Alarie House was made for. She was all froth and beauty, her charm lighting her from the inside. If Isla was functional and unalluring as a round of bread, Carina was a work of patisserie. But take any girl in the world, and there was something that could be ridiculed.

They could have gone after anything about Carina. Carina was the kind of curvy Isla had once imagined princesses being, but she could have grown up being bullied for her grasa parda. She was kind, which meant she might have been a sensitive child, quick to tears, and her classmates might have made a blood sport out of trying to make her cry. She could have loved singing and not been able to carry a tune in a velvet-lined box. Short as she was, she might have had an early, awkward growth spurt. She might have been tripping over her own limbs in the compulsory ballet classes meant to give society girls grace.

"Why do you think I wanted to come here so badly?" Carina asked. "The name on this house, when we leave it, it's more important than any other name we'll ever have. More important than the name my mother and father gave me. More important than the name I'll take from my husband."

Carina's words stirred the hope in Isla's chest so brightly that it stung.

"You think you don't belong here," Carina said. "I could tell the first day we met."

It left Isla's throat tight, knowing her self-conscious flinch was that obvious.

"I don't know why," Carina said. "Maybe you think your sister's too hard an act to follow. I'd probably feel that way if I were you."

It was true.

It also wasn't the half of it.

"Whatever it is, it's not just you. None of us would be here if we didn't have empty space in us." Carina put an arm around Isla. It was a sort of half hug, and it made her perfume, sweet as candied violets, drift over both of them. "This whole time, you've been wondering if you're safe here, if we're safe here. But it's never been about that."

Carina looked out at the land running toward the dusk-tinged mountains. The nearest road was close to the horizon, a matte ribbon that buckled and shone from the heat. Behind them, the front gate was a dark whisper against the pale land.

But Isla was looking at Carina, this girl who woke up early to polish her white shoes, lest a single scuff declare her unworthy of her place here. This girl, who took furious notes in class. This girl, who wanted the Alarie blessing more than she wanted her own name. She wasn't just froth and light. She knew what she'd come here for. She'd gone after it with single-minded force that could have cleaved a diamond.

"We don't come here to be safe," Carina said. "We come here so we can earn something that will keep us safe for the rest of our lives."

FORTY

"**W**HEN GIVING A DINNER party"—Eduarda had them all standing around the dining room table— "you give yourself the greatest chance of success when your guests number more than the Graces but less than the Muses." She gave them all an expectant look.

Carina's hand flew up. Her fingertips reached for the ceiling, as though trying to compensate for how much shorter her arms were than taller girls'.

"Yes." Eduarda extended an acknowledging hand in Carina's direction.

"More than three, less than nine?" Carina said.

"Precisely," Eduarda said. "But speak your answers with confidence. Be proud of what you know."

Isla still hadn't heard from Renata. And nothing at the house had changed. Not even Isla trying to tear apart the floor in the fevered haze of her dreams. Paz was gone but Renata hadn't reappeared, and Isla's nightmares still made her hands something outside her.

And she needed Paz to tell her why.

When Isla reached the workshop, there Paz was, marking up a rough gem. She did not seem afraid. She did not seem surprised that Isla had come. Her posture was languorous as a boy leaning against a doorframe.

She had on her usual ink-black trousers, the sleeves of her shirt cuffed up. The dark cord of her braid fell over her shoulder. Something like a riding jacket was thrown over one of the many weathered tables that had been abandoned here.

There was something unkempt about her. Her shirt was wrinkled, and pieces were coming loose from her braid. A lace frill of white trimmed her hairline, soap she hadn't fully washed off her face. There were half-drunk glasses of water, half-finished cups of tea, and half-eaten apples scattered across the workstations, as though Paz kept forgetting them partway through.

"It's called a scratch ring," Paz said, "in case you didn't know."

Paz still hadn't looked up. Only the slight incline of her head confirmed that she was talking about Renata's diamond ring.

"Famous women throughout history have had them.

Elizabeth I. Mary, Queen of Scots. Casanova's lover Henriette." Paz made little flicks of a felt marking pen. "They would write letters or poems by scratching them out on a windowpane."

A chill crawled over the back of Isla's neck.

So Paz had seen Isla's etchings on the Alarie House windows.

"It's more permanent than writing on paper. A window lasts longer." Paz switched to another rough and a graphite pencil. "But it's also more fragile. Glass can break at any time, and then the words are lost, all at once."

Isla's fingers touched the ring, making to pull it off. "You can have it if you tell me what happened with my sister."

"I don't need your diamond. I have my own." Paz held up a rough stone that looked little different from broken glass, but that would glitter like water once it was cut.

"What about this?" Isla lifted the star sapphire away from her neck. "If you want this back, tell me what you did to her, to all of them."

To all of us.

It had gotten to Isla too. She'd felt it, and it had thrilled her as many times as it had frightened her.

The sapphire swung lightly on its dark cord. The motion drew Paz's eye, just for a split second, and Isla caught the flinch of Paz wanting it back. Then Paz retracted her expression back to neutral.

"I don't have anything to tell you." Paz went back to the graphite pencil and the rough she was marking.

I don't have anything to tell you. Somehow it was even worse than *I don't have to tell you anything.* It was more final. It broached even less objection.

All the spite and power drained out of Isla. It was the awful letdown of playing the best hand she had and finding that her opponent didn't even care to sit down at the table.

"If you don't want to tell me what you did, tell me how to stop it." Isla sounded more desperate now. She could hear it. She was losing ground with every word.

Paz took her time answering. She was considering one aluminum scribe, and then another. "Those girls at that house are doing exactly what they're expected to do."

"It's dangerous," Isla said. "You know that."

"Of course it's dangerous. Beauty is dangerous." Paz surveyed the roughs before her. "Torbernite is green as emeralds. It forms into shapes like trees. Forests of gemstones. It's also radioactive. Cerussite has a higher dispersion value than diamonds. Absolutely stunning internal fire." She sounded like she was musing to herself. "When it's cut properly, it looks like a thousand rainbows inside a shell of crystal. And do you know what it's made of? White lead ore. It's poisonous. And let us not forget beryllium. One of the most toxic elements known to man, yet there are no emeralds without it."

Paz held a rough up to the light. "The most wondrous things you will ever see hold the most dangerous poison." She turned the raw mineral. "The most remarkable beauty is made of the deadliest secrets."

Light gathered in the center as though the stone was breathing.

"You can't change that," Paz said. "I can't either."

There was no smirk, no taunting, not even fear. Only resignation.

Whatever Paz had done, she'd lost control of it. The Alarie girls had taken it and made it their own.

Thanks to the Alarie girls, Paz was now nothing. She looked like a ghost, a column of smoke, an apparition of black hair and the gauzy white of her shirt.

Isla had come here for answers. And the Alarie girls knew more than Paz.

The Alarie girls knew everything.

FORTY-ONE

CARINA'S ROOM WAS A planet where lace grew like moss on a forest floor. It was an enchanted world where frills fluttered in the breeze from the window, looking like sea creatures.

The ruffled covers on Carina's half-made bed were as layered and off-kilter as a wedding cake sliding off a table. The dresser was crowded with perfumes, hair ribbons, powder puffs, silver hand mirrors. Her wardrobe creaked open, threatening to spill tulle everywhere like pastel clouds.

Sure hands, the hands of older girls, touched Isla's hair and face. Isla would have once been afraid they would consume her, pull her into the dark. But they were only polishing her, refining her.

They held dresses up to her to find her exact best shade of

white. They put no makeup on her but a blush the same pink as her lips. They arranged her hair as though the wind itself had swirled it into a gentle knot at the nape of her neck.

Being an Alarie girl papered over everything. It put a gloss on life. It was rich as velvet and obscuring as varnish.

It meant nothing could touch Isla. Not Paz. Not the gash in the foyer. Not the girls whose voices echoed through her nightmares years later.

A shimmer of gold swirled in Carina's mirror. The longer Isla looked, the more clearly the form emerged.

Here she was again, the girl with the hair made of liquid gold. But this time Isla did not recoil from her. This time, Isla saw her for the beautifully perfected creature she was.

But how do I get her back? Isla couldn't even speak the question. She was breathing it out, and it clung to the mirror like the thinnest layer of fog. *How do I get my sister back?*

The girl's face had been shaped with as many facets as a brilliant cut stone. Her body was translucent as quartz, but her facets threw the light around, multiplying it, so she seemed made of light. Her teeth were diamonds cut sharp as the points of solitaires.

Become one of us, she breathed back, her words a faint, whirring whisper, *and you'll never have lost her in the first place.*

Between the bite of her back teeth, white light refracted into colors.

Her voice sounded like the echo of Renata's voice.

It sounded like Carina's voice.

And it sounded like the other girls in this room.

Maybe the whole time, it hadn't just been Renata's whisper in these walls.

Maybe it had been every Alarie girl who had ever come through this house, whispering to every Alarie girl who came after them. The thought was a bracing thrill. It would mean Isla was the same as the other girls here. She heard what they heard. She dreamed what they dreamed. She was as unquestionably a girl as any of them.

"We don't simply polish ourselves for fun"—this time a voice from the room, not from inside the mirror. One of the older girls was setting a stray lock of Isla's hair in its proper place. She had a voice like honeyed tea, like Eduarda's might have been before it took on the royal lilt of a finishing school instructor. "You know what they say. The polished surface deflects the arrow."

That was the truth of it. If you shone fiercely enough, nothing could pierce you. Even light could do nothing but glance off a brilliantly shining girl. Nothing could touch a girl whose flesh was jewels set over platinum bones.

The diamond-mouthed girl smiled, and Isla felt herself smiling. Isla was the reflection, not her, and that made them both girls cut from diamond.

It made them both flawless.

It made them both as hard and sharp as the glittering stone their flesh had become.

FORTY-TWO

THE GASH IN THE foyer yawned open.

It was a broken ribbon in the floor, like the stripe in a piece of selenite.

The tile and sub-flooring split open wide enough to show the sparkling earth underneath. The crystals were small and jagged, like the crack in the floor was a mouth that had grown a million glittering teeth.

Eduarda paused just before the steps down into the sunken atrium. She took a breath as slowly as if she were drinking in the honeysuckle on the spring air. "How lovely," she sighed, with a satisfaction so complete, anyone would have thought she'd commissioned this alteration to the foyer.

By that night, the gash had spread into a small chasm.

It reached from one end of the sunken atrium to the other. Crystals coated the darkness in red, blue, and purple.

When Isla went to look, Carina was at the mezzanine railing. She stared down at the gash, her face more unnerved than Isla had ever seen.

Carina had never seemed wary of heights, not when she was on the roof, not when she was climbing into the chandelier, not when she was perched on the railing. But the way her eyes fixed on the floor now made her seem more afraid of that glittering darkness than she'd ever been of falling.

"There's nothing to be frightened of," Isla said.

Carina looked around. When she found Isla, she seemed to settle, at least a little. But her nervousness still tinted the air around her.

Carina had calmed Isla so many times, starting with that safety pin offered under the table.

This was Isla's chance to return the favor.

"Watch." Isla ran down the stairs. Static sparked in the dry air between the carpet and her feet.

"What are you doing?" Carina whispered.

Isla paused at the bottom of the stairs and looked up. "It's all right." She leapt down the chilled tile of the atrium steps, her white nightgown lapping the air behind her.

Carina gasped, her small hands reaching over the railing.

"I told you." Isla stepped into the gash. The depth of the colors made the crystals look like an ocean on another planet. "There's nothing to be afraid of."

The edges sent pain through the bottoms of her feet. But after so many days of stiff dress shoes pinching her toes, it didn't faze her.

In the upper corner of Isla's peripheral vision, more girls gathered at the railing. Their whispers were dainty as the ribbons in their hair.

Pain shot through the arches of Isla's feet. It was sharp as the diffraction of white light inside a diamond. It was pain breaking into colors.

But it was also invigorating. Isla was walking on raw jewels. She was walking on fractured light. She was an Alarie girl, graceful enough to stroll across jagged minerals as though they were level ground.

The other girls looked on, eyes wide. But they weren't judging her. Even out of the corner of her eye, Isla could tell they weren't.

They were mesmerized. They were as thrilled as Isla was.

The pain in her feet rushed into her ankles. It shot up through her body. By the time it reached her rib cage, it was exhilaration. She was Eduarda. She was Renata. She was Mauricia. She was every flawless girl.

The blur of a yellow nightgown rushed down the stairs like a filmy comet.

"Isla." Carina reached out and grabbed her arm.

Isla felt her own mouth open. It did not feel like her mouth, but a copy of the gash under her feet, yawning open into a glittering maw.

She screamed so sharply it rang through the chandelier above them. She felt the jagged, glittering edges lining the inside of her cheeks like salt flowers along a shoreline. Her tongue was a garnet. Her soft palate was coated in a hundred thousand tiny facets. Her mouth was a geode, broken open and filled with crystals.

Pure fear registered on Carina's face. She drew her hand back.

The scream cut out in Isla's throat.

Isla's mouth was her mouth again. She felt it shaping into a reassuring smile.

Carina looked timid as a rabbit. But she did not run. She only looked down at Isla's feet and said in a small voice, "You're bleeding."

Isla followed Carina's eyes.

Blood slicked the crystals.

"Oh." Isla's laugh bubbled through the word.

Carina saw blood and thought it was cause for alarm, when it was no more cause for alarm than the gash itself. Everything was fine here. Everything here was beautiful.

The chandelier went still and silent above their heads, floating like a jeweled jellyfish.

"Don't worry; it doesn't hurt," Isla said, because it didn't. Everything was too lovely for anything to hurt. "Here."

Isla held out her hand.

Carina looked down at her own bare feet, at Isla's, at the sparkling gash in the floor.

"You're a pink diamond," Isla whispered. "You're too precious to get scratched."

Carina's expression relaxed and opened.

She took Isla's hand. With every watching eye on her, she stepped into the chasm.

Her first step was cautious. Her face showed the pinch of the crystals against the soles of her feet.

Isla held on to her. She gave her an encouraging nod.

With her next step, Carina's fear became elation. Isla could see it.

With each step, Isla left blood on the dark jewels, but she barely felt it. And when liquid gold came up from the ground, she couldn't tell the difference between that and her own blood.

The more girls joined them, the more girls walked on the jagged surface, the more gold came up from the floor. It seeped between the crystals. Around where Isla stood, ribbons of her blood streaked the gold like the veins in an agate slice. Drops looked like rubies in ring settings.

But that blood wasn't hers. It couldn't be hers.

They were gold-plated girls with raw garnet hearts and bloodstone tongues. The water in their bodies was simply the water trapped inside opal.

This was what was under the ground, what she'd been looking for in her nightmares. This was what her hands had been searching for when they broke things apart.

Her heart wasn't under this floor. It was her blood,

because she was an Alarie girl, and there was no telling her own blood from molten gold. There was no telling her own bones from carved opal, her own flesh from brown moonstone. There was no telling the chasm in the floor from her own crystalline mouth.

FORTY-THREE

THE LETTER ARRIVED without a return address.

Inside was a single card, the stationery heavy as starched fabric. A few lines of familiar cursive looped over the page, clean black on stark white.

The note was worded so impeccably that Alba Alarie could have scripted it herself. It invited Isla to afternoon tea, at an address she had never seen before.

She had done it.

She had followed her sister's path here, and she had done it with such perfection that her sister had summoned her.

FORTY-FOUR

ISLA TRIPLE-CHECKED THE ADDRESS. By distance, she hadn't gone far, but it seemed an entire world away.

Where the Alarie House was all clean lines, black trim, white stucco, this manor looked both faded and distinguished with age. It was set back from the road by a sloping lawn, and instead of a looming gate, low drystone walls bounded the yard. Lichen and ivy patched the fieldstone, and bunches of flowers jutted in all directions, so dense they seemed gathered by hand.

It looked like the kind of country estate owned by a family who had no vocation other than inheriting money. Most likely not their primary residence. This grand, stately house had the air of being a property they would nonchalantly refer to as their *summer cottage*.

The lawn had been so recently mown there were bands in the grass. It wrapped around the house and waved over the land, toward a back garden shaded by beech woods.

The grounds looked set for a party. Pastel macarons were stacked like a wedding cake. The caramel on a croquembouche shone where the sun struck it. In an enormous punch bowl, purple and yellow flowers drifted on a sea of coral pink.

It looked like a party. But it was so strangely quiet that the girls could have been garden sculptures. A group of them sat impassive around a wooden table, under the shade of the house's eaves. They all wore black velvet dresses, and their sleeves moved with the breeze more than they themselves moved, so the fabric looked like black petunias and black zinnias.

The most extravagant motions they made were slow, dainty bites of madeleines or polvorones. All were so thickly coated with powdered sugar it looked like the act of eating them would leave a snowdrift over their perfect black dresses. But not a wisp of powdered sugar touched the dark velvet.

The quilts thrown over the lawn were as spotless and neat as bedspreads in a guest room. Girls in white dresses fit for a debutante ball had arranged their skirts so they fanned out over the ground. They took sips from teacups so delicate the light came through.

One girl sat directly on the grass, her skirt brilliant white against the chlorophyll green. She was smiling in a way that was both more and less unsettling when Isla saw she was playing with paper dolls. They looked like the ones at the Alarie House.

"Isla," said a voice as delicate as a teacup being set down on a saucer.

Isla turned toward the sound.

Renata's smile had a sharpness behind it, a gleam that reminded Isla of the sister she'd had before either of them ever enrolled in finishing school.

FORTY-FIVE

"BEAUTIFUL, ISN'T IT?" RENATA lifted her gaze toward the trees. "It belongs to the family of one of our fellow graduates. For a few years she's been opening it up to those of us whose relatives have been less than understanding about our growth."

Isla let her sister get the jab in. She couldn't blame Renata. Isla hadn't understood, not until now.

"It's a sort of midpoint between the Alarie House and going out into society," Renata said. "It's very peaceful here, and she's terribly generous to share it with us."

Magazines showed the Alarie girls who became princesses, First Ladies, the wives of industry kings. But maybe these were the girls no one heard about, the ones who had gotten so comfortable being cloistered that the rest of the world held nothing for them.

Renata looked made to sit on a manicured lawn in a chiffon dress. The dark brown of her hair had been softly arranged, and there was a subtle blush on her cheeks. She was luminous against the sun and the green. But there was a blankness to her, a vacancy behind her eyes.

"It's so dull to begin with apologies." Renata poured tea into a second cup. "But I do owe you one. I don't know what came over me." Renata handed the cup and saucer to Isla.

Isla took it.

"You must despise me." Renata laughed so lightly she sounded as though she was apologizing for wearing white to an engagement party.

"No," Isla said. "Of course I don't."

"How are the girls?" Renata topped off her own cup. "Is Laureana still there? And Beth, how is Beth?"

That was it? No further discussion of what had passed between them? Nothing else about Renata leaving?

"You know Abuela's combing the earth for you, right?" Isla asked.

"I'm sorry. I didn't mean to worry anyone." Renata poured milk into her tea.

When had *that* changed? Abuela had always taught them to pour in milk before tea, before coffee, before anything that could stain. It was how you took care of your teacups. Was this an affect of finishing school girls, making some kind of point that you were above worrying about staining?

"Then why not tell her where you are?" Isla asked. "Or at least tell her you're all right?"

Renata pinched the handle of the teacup between her gloved fingers. "I was hoping you might do that."

So this wasn't even about Renata wanting to see Isla. This wasn't about Renata's relief that Isla finally understood what she'd found at the Alarie House.

She wanted Isla to be her messenger.

"I've written to her," Renata said. " "She knows I'm where I want to be. She also knows she can't make me come home. So it would mean a great deal to me if you would reassure her that I truly am fine."

"When did you write to her?" Isla asked.

Renata took a dainty sip. "When I realized what a stir she was causing. Asking everyone about me."

"Can you blame her?" Isla asked.

"It's all very overblown." Renata looked off into where the trees thickened, the space between carpeted with bluebells. "Sometimes a lady needs time to herself."

"You disappeared in the middle of the night," Isla said, her voice smaller, her anger tamped back. Her voice was something outside herself. It had neither the power she wanted it to nor the finishing school grace she was supposed to be learning. "And for what? This is the Alarie House but with no classes. What's the point? So you all can just sit around here like you're under glass?"

"Better a polished jewel under glass than a rough stone in the dirt," Renata said.

Isla felt her whole body recoiling. "What does that mean?"

Renata sighed. "I didn't mean anything by it."

"Like hell you didn't. What exactly is the dirt supposed to be?" Isla had been sitting with her legs and her skirt arranged in a mirror of Renata's, but now she was on her knees, half-way to standing. "You think I'm a rough stone? You think I'm unpolished? Still? After all this?"

"I didn't say anything of the sort."

Isla had spent her whole life feeling less than Renata, and it had forever made her feel indebted to Renata for claiming her as a sister. But now Isla felt vicious and competitive. She wasn't less than Renata anymore. Or at least she wouldn't be soon. That was the promise of the Alarie House. Even with her body that was not what a girl's body was supposed to be, the Alarie House was making her into a jewel of a girl. She had the crystal-cut scars to prove it.

"I am doing everything you did there," Isla said.

"Of course you are." Renata's expression was so encouraging that Isla wanted to slap it off her face.

"And I did what you couldn't do," Isla said. "I got the poison out of that house."

Renata gave the far edge of the lawn a regretful look. "I

wish I hadn't worried you. But Abuela wouldn't understand this. To her, the only way to live is to be all of you at once. To her, it's very simple, when the truth is, it's anything but. Some parts of us are meant to be shown fully lit. Others are best remaining discreetly in shadow."

"What"—Isla quickly stopped herself from adding in *the hell*—"are you talking about?"

Renata tilted her head, considering.

"Do you know how you've always liked huevos divorciados?" she asked.

What did any of this have to do with breakfast food?

"It's a little like that," Renata said. "The dish is better for having the two different sauces on two different sides. The division between them is part of the magic."

For the past few minutes, Isla had wanted nothing but for Renata to look at her. Now that Renata did, there was little behind her eyes. Only that lovely, flattening gaze that the Alarie sisters had and that the most refined Alarie House enrollees learned to imitate. It was as though everything in the world was beautiful and everything that wasn't could be leveled under their cheerful decorum.

Renata was right. She was an adult. Abuela couldn't make her come home. Isla certainly couldn't make her do anything.

But Renata also couldn't make Isla listen to this.

Isla got up and went to the dessert table. Carina loved sweets, and she was covering for both their chores in her absence. The least Isla could do was bring her back something.

But there was also the edge of something else, how much she wanted to rip apart everything here that was pretty and proper.

Renata rose from the grass. "Isla."

Isla shoved a confetti of pastel macarons into a cloth napkin and then into her purse.

Renata stood on the other side of the table. "Did you know that opals, quite literally, hold water?"

"Yes." Isla wasn't in the mood for her sister to teach her facts they'd learned from the same grandmother. "I did."

"Then you know that every opal has water molecules inside it," Renata said. "Water becomes caught in the gem, as though frozen."

Isla broke the profiteroles out of their caramel shells.

"Without water, opal has no fire," Renata said. "No dazzle. Each one is different, but they all have the same secrets."

"Yes, water," Isla said. "I've got it."

"Not just water." Renata set her hands on the table. "Order. In the finest opal, the play of light seems chaotic. Random. When the truth is that the molecules are arranged neatly, evenly."

Isla snapped the whole upper third off the croquem-bouche. When a few girls looked over, she stared back at them, daring them to say anything.

"That precise arrangement allows the illusion of all colors," Renata said. "Blue, green, and pink like iridescent snow, all the way to the orange and red ones that look like flames. It's all because of those two things, water and order."

Isla wrapped the profiteroles in a napkin and shoved them into her purse. She wanted to be a shameless girl pilfering sweets under a perfect blue sky. She wanted to shock the watching girls.

She wanted to shock Renata.

Renata stood where she was, the wind lifting her hair off her shoulders. "The more orderly the arrangement, the more dazzling the opal appears. Actual randomness within the stone would make an opal flat, dull as doused embers. It's the organization of the mineral that makes rainbows. Fire. Sparkle. Play of color."

Isla emptied a candy dish into her purse. She looked right at Renata while she did it, to make the point, but it left her aim a little off. Candy spilled around her feet and scattered into the grass.

"Without order," Renata said, "without keeping the different parts of ourselves where they're meant to be, we cannot sparkle. Diamonds sparkle because of their precise configuration of carbon atoms. Even if you smash a diamond, it breaks evenly. You obliterate it, and still it retains its order."

They were words Paz might have introduced into Renata's brain like the color element in a stone.

"She's gone," Isla said.

Renata's face was as unmoving as the surface of the punch bowl.

"Paz is gone," Isla said. "You don't have to be afraid of her anymore."

Renata blinked at her. "Who?"

The girl with the paper dolls started laughing and ripping up the paper clothes.

"Paz." With increasing frustration, Isla described her, the braid down her back, the perfectly ironed trousers, the shirts tailored with precise ruffles, the sapphire that was once tied around her neck.

"I knew the names of all the girls who were there when I was," Renata said, with a measure of pride as modest as a pinch of salt. "I didn't know any Paz. And I certainly didn't know anyone the Alarie sisters allowed to wear pants."

Renata's laugh was light and disbelieving, as though Isla had made an absurd joke. *Pants at a finishing school, and at the Alarie House no less? Can you even imagine?*

The girl with the paper dolls laughed harder. The paper women in her hands looked just like her, ten copies of her in flat, glossed cardstock. Isla had barely noticed the resemblance until the girl started ripping up the paper dolls themselves, cackling as she tore their heads from their bodies.

Isla took them out of her hands. "Stop."

The girl screamed. Her mouth was lined with red-purple crystals, her tongue a ghostly phantom in the stone. The back of her throat lit up like she'd swallowed a solar flare.

It wasn't beautiful.

It was monstrous.

Not because her mouth looked like a gem-filled crack in the ground.

Not because she was screaming.

Because she was holding some bright raging thing at the core of her, and it was burning her up from the inside.

There was a ring around the scream, an echo. As it grew louder, Isla realized the second scream was coming from Renata. The inside of her mouth was dark as a well, and her tongue was a red crystal knife.

Isla was no longer touching anything or anyone. She had dropped the paper dolls. She wasn't stopping the girl from reaching for them again. The girl with the paper dolls had even stopped screaming.

But Renata didn't stop. A smile lit her eyes and twisted the corners of the cavern where her mouth had been. She looked thrilled, gleeful at the wrath streaming out of her. And she locked her radiant, terrifying stare on Isla.

Renata's mouth was a field of dark stars, bending all light around her. Her throat held the molten center of the earth. She would burn up anything she breathed on.

And she wanted Isla to know it. Isla could see it in the vicious delight filling her eyes.

It was that unyielding glee that made Isla run across the grass for the road. And as she did, Renata's screaming broke into the skipping pitch of a laugh.

FORTY-SIX

ALL OF THIS WAS wrong. The Alarie House
was supposed to make Isla and Renata as much
the same as they could ever be. It was supposed
to fix what had broken between them.

By the time Isla got back to the Alarie House, her lungs
were tight and hitching as though she'd run the whole way.
Whatever she was still missing, it had to be in there. She'd rip
it out of the walls if she needed to.

Isla went for the nearest door. Whatever she had to do,
she'd do it. She'd smile until her cheeks cracked into facets.
She'd prance along the roofline with her eyes shut. She'd shred
a thousand paper dolls that looked exactly like her.

But when Isla took her first step into the Alarie House,
the sound of a hundred breaking glasses propelled her back.

Then the sound kept going. More glasses broke. The noise blew out from the center of the house. It came with a rush of air and the shimmering whisper of crushed diamonds.

That was when Isla knew. Even as she was still running, her steps crunching over crushed jewels, she knew.

The chandelier in the middle of the foyer had broken into a galaxy. The blue topaz and emeralds had splintered into pieces of the sea or sky. The sapphires and garnets shattered into nebulas. The milky opals broke like moons crashing to Earth, spilling out their light.

The girl in the middle of the fallen chandelier wore a pink dress. The different shades of rose made her a ghostly version of Fragonard's girl on a swing.

But the swing's ropes hadn't caught her. There had been no soft green foliage to break her fall. There was only the hard, warped metal of bent candle slips, and the only thing to catch her had been the floor, split open into that shimmering geode.

Isla's heart cracked like the chandelier's central column. She dropped next to Carina, crushing pieces of broken gems under her knees. She tried to scream Carina's name, but it came out as a choked whisper.

Carina's hair had tangled on the castings. The pendeloques from the chandelier jabbed into her body. The culets had slashed at her skin. Her dress and the deep green of the heliotropes were splashed with identical shades of red.

A point of molten gold dripped off the end of the fallen finial.

"I told you," Carina whispered, the words quiet as wisps of smoke.

She looked at the ceiling as though she could see through it. Her expression was peaceful as a saint contemplating heaven.

"I knew it." Carina's eyes moved to Isla. "You didn't want to like me."

As she spoke, red glittered on her neck.

A string of rubies had thrown a slash of shining red across her throat. "But you do."

FORTY-SEVEN

"**WHITE PAPER IS BEST**," Alba said. "Plain, heavy stock. Anything more ostentatious is tacky."

A memory pinched Isla, Carina fanning out her leaves of pink, blue, and yellow stationery, saying, *Behold my contraband.*

"Write in the easy manner with which you would speak." Alba walked the room. "As if you are sitting across from the recipient. Bernarda, no underlining. It makes well wishes sound sarcastic."

Another thought of Carina intruded, Carina holding gold-edged notecards with the scandalous glee of nude photographs.

"Viviana, dear, don't tell your cousin you hope she'll

have a 'memorable' wedding," Alba said. "Especially not with 'memorable' in quotations. Ladies, underlining and quotations do not emphasize your point. They undercut it. Think of telling your mother you'll be on your 'best' behavior. It sounds as if she might find you entering an ax-throwing contest at the nearest tavern."

They kept coming, the thoughts of what Carina would be doing if she was sitting at the desk next to Isla's. She'd be making faces until the moment Alba turned around, at which point Carina would be back at her writing, eyes downturned in a perfect display of concentration.

"Or telling your friend her fiancé is *truly handsome*, underlined," Alba said. "She'll think what you really mean is that you've seen lovelier heads on the fish at the market stall."

Next was the memory of Eduarda correcting Carina in the fond way she could only ever correct a girl who reminded her of herself. *Carina, dear, stop swinging your feet. You are sitting, not performing at the Folies-Bergère.*

But Carina wasn't here, and the rest of them were. They were all having their morning lesson, as though nothing had happened. The doctors had taken Carina away. Then, last Isla had heard, her nearest relatives had taken her home.

No one spoke of it. Not between classes. Not at the dining room table.

It was a regrettable accident, it seemed, and no one considered it worth dwelling on any further than that.

Nothing was worth dwelling on except the most trivial details of comportment.

"How, you might be wondering, is one to hold a glass, a refreshment plate, and a napkin all at once?" Eduarda mused at the start of afternoon instruction. "It really is easier than you might think. Who will come up and help me demonstrate?"

Isla sat in her chair, arms folded, body coiled tight. She wasn't volunteering. Not for this, not for anything.

Eduarda showed one of the girls how to hold the stem of a glass between two fingers. The plate was wedged between her thumb and forefinger. "And the napkin just under the plate, held with the third finger," Eduarda said. "Yes, very good. And accomplished with the necessary skill to avoid giving the room an obscene gesture. Well done."

If Eduarda wanted obscene, all she had to do was look at this room. If Eduarda felt anything, she showed none of it. They were all pretending there wasn't one fewer of them. There had barely been a shift in mood.

The older girls held their peaceful demeanors as they moved from tutorial to tutorial. They were dignified ladies carrying on after an unfortunate occurrence. And the newer girls followed their lead.

"And speaking of eating," Eduarda said after she dismissed her volunteer, "must I remind you not to indulge in patisserie over your host's carpets? Crumbs can damage a good rug as easily as wax dripping from a candle."

That was it. Crumbs and candle wax. Nothing more disagreeable could exist here for long. All unpleasantness had been, quite literally, swept away. The pieces of the broken chandelier had been gone by the next morning. Now there was nothing but the jeweled gash in the floor and a dangling cord where the chandelier had been.

"For conversation," Eduarda said, "museum exhibits, public gardens, some local industry, these are safe, neutral topics."

Anger coiled inside Isla.

"No marigolds in the hair except on appropriate holidays," Eduarda said. "No red roses unless you want a gentleman to think you're a seductress."

It trembled like a spring.

"And for the love of everything, no lilies."

Isla had to get out of this room.

"Even if you're rude enough to ignore how many are sensitive to the smell, I cannot tell you how many shirts and draperies I've seen ruined by the pollen."

Isla went out into the far-too-perfect day and sat on one of the far-too-pretty benches.

First, she had failed Renata by not staying here in the first place. And now she had failed Carina. Once, Isla had been the one pulling Carina back. Then she'd become the one leading Carina forward, getting her to walk on sharp edges.

A shadow grayed the white wrought iron. A faintly storm-blue skirt lapped at the bench.

"May I join you?" Luisa Alarie asked.

Isla probably should have been honored.

Her shrug was something short of ladylike, but it was more ladylike than anything that might come out of her mouth.

"You don't have to be in class." Luisa sat down. "If you're not feeling well."

Isla straightened her posture but did not speak. She didn't want to talk to any of the Alarie sisters. All of this had happened on their watch. They had refused to see any of it.

Luisa looked out over the gravel paths. "What was she doing up there?"

It didn't sound so much like a question as a lament.

Isla looked at Luisa, wondering if she'd really just heard what she'd heard from the eldest Alarie sister. Luisa Alarie had brought up something everyone else was avoiding talking about.

"I've wanted to take it down for years." Luisa shook her head at the horizon. "I always thought it was dangerous to have something that beautiful somewhere that high. Of course someone would want to touch it. How could anyone help it? It's in our blood. Humans are partial to things that sparkle because they look like the sun reflecting off water. They look like something we need to survive."

Luisa seemed to wind herself down, pull herself back. "But our mother insisted it stay. She said it was tradition."

The way Luisa said *tradition* was the closest she'd ever sounded to bitter.

The official story from Carina's family was that she'd

recover, that the bleeding had stopped, that her bones would knit. But Luisa's face looked so regretful that Isla wondered if Carina might be about to die. She had looked like she had as many broken bones as a rose-cut diamond had star facets. Any one of them could give her the fever that killed her.

"You care about your friend a great deal," Luisa said. Not a question.

To call Carina her friend seemed an understatement. Carina had been her first window into what this place could mean. With little more than a safety pin between her fingers, she had told Isla that she could have everything that any other girl had.

Luisa laughed lightly, fondly, and it was a sound so out of place that it made Isla want to kick at the gravel under the bench.

"You're so much like your sister," Luisa said.

Isla's shoes came to a stop. She stared at Luisa. The whole problem had always been how little Isla was like Renata. Sure, they could pull the same pranks, raise the same eyebrows, but Isla would never live up to her sister. She didn't have Renata's breasts or height or hips or waistline. She didn't have Renata's conviction that only those who loved her were worth considering. She didn't even have the same pieces to herself as Renata, the same organs, the same cells.

You're so much like your sister. Isla wanted to catch the words in her hands so she could keep them, and she wanted to tear them apart to show what a lie they were.

"Carina was one of her favorites too, when she was here," Luisa said. "One of many things the two of you have in common."

"You think I'm like Renata? I don't even know her anymore." A boldness stirred up in Isla like sediment in a river. "What happened when she was here?"

Luisa's posture shifted. She blinked as though surprised to be asked something so obvious. "Your sister committed herself to her studies. Has anyone implied otherwise?"

Isla dug her shoes into the damp dirt. "What happened when my sister was here?"

"She proved herself a credit to this school. I've never heard anyone say a bad word about her. I assure you I wouldn't hear it."

Isla tamped down the scream in her throat. She spoke in a measured tone. "What is happening in this house?"

Luisa considered a scuff on the white wrought iron. "Some of the most impressive gem settings are held together with nothing more than tension," she said. "That goes for the settings in the house too. So many of them, no mortar at all, simply held in place with precisely set gold prongs. Tension may not be pleasant, but it yields exceptional results."

She sounded like Renata.

No. Renata sounded like the Alarie sisters.

How could the Alarie sisters ever find fault with who she had become? She was just like them. They could never even imagine Renata coming after her own sister with a letter opener. They could fathom that no more than girls dancing on roofs at midnight, screaming with caverns in place of their mouths.

"Something's wrong here," Isla said. "What's happening in this house, you have to stop it."

"It's a foolish woman, of any age, to think she can control anyone else." Luisa rose from the bench. "She does well enough to control herself."

So they did know.

The Alarie sisters had some idea of what the girls here did at night, what they became at night. And they did nothing to stop it. They did not want to know, and so they turned their attention away as soon as the lamps were lowered for the night.

This was what they would always do. They would gloss over everything. Girls could be shoving each other off the roof, and they would still pretend everything was cordial as always. They would keep themselves so ignorant that they would manage to be shocked when a girl fell two stories to the tile floor, encased in a net of jewels.

Isla knew this. She hated Luisa and her sisters for it. And yet she could not reconcile it with the troubled look that now appeared on Luisa's face.

"Have you heard anything from Paz?" Luisa asked.

She looked not just troubled but worried.

"No," Isla said. This time there was no thrill in the lie.

"That girl"—Luisa considered the gravel at her feet—"she

does nothing without dramatic flair. If she'd decided she was through with the curriculum here, I'm sure she would have left a scathing note, on good stationery no less." Luisa looked up. "Will you let me know if you do hear from her? She seemed fond of you. She might write to you instead of us."

It was such an unadorned request, the worry so close to that of an aunt or an older cousin. Isla could hate this woman all she wanted. She still heard herself saying, "Yes."

Luisa gave a nod of gratitude.

"I don't know how many girls have come through this house in the last few years," Luisa said. "Alba probably does. But I do know that sometimes I wish certain girls had studied here at the same time, girls who missed each other entirely but who I think might have been a good influence. And I've thought that about Paz." Luisa sighed. "I do wish Paz had had the chance to spend some time around your sister."

The unease forming inside Isla fractured. It splintered into more pieces than she could hold.

"That's not to say I don't think you yourself can be a good influence on the other girls, because I think you will be," Luisa said. "But for Paz, I think she could use someone like Renata to look up to. She has no sisters, and I think an older sister figure would have been a steadying influence on her, the way Renata has undoubtedly been for you."

The words were still making their way into Isla's brain. But Luisa was already off toward the house, her steps barely crunching as she walked across the gravel.

The Alarie sisters turned their backs to what went on at night. They didn't want to know what their lovely finishing school girls did, and what they convinced themselves and each other to do.

But they truly had no idea what Isla had done to Paz.

Now Isla herself wasn't even sure what she'd done to Paz.

Paz had proven herself afraid of nothing. Not shocking the Alarie sisters. Not defying the very idea of what an Alarie girl was meant to be. Not the point of a marquise-cut stone against her throat. Not taking the blame for the madness of a girl she'd never even met. Not even Isla threatening to shove her off a roof.

A girl shedding unnecessary fear moved more easily through the world. Abuela and Renata had both tried to teach Isla that.

But when a girl lost all her fear, she became dangerous without even knowing it. All Isla had to do was think of Carina to know what happened when a girl was afraid of absolutely nothing. A girl who was afraid of nothing could destroy anything, starting with herself.

FORTY-EIGHT

ISLA'S STEPS CUT THROUGH the dark, her dress billowing out behind her as she retraced the route to the workshop.

A shiver of light swirled in the air between wild olive trees. The longer Isla looked, the more the light took shape.

She was out here, the girl made of faceted diamond. Her hair was gold that flowed like water. She was too exact, with edges too sharp, to be beautiful. She was something more powerful than that. She was stunning. She was awe-inspiring.

When she smiled, her diamond face began to crack, first the corners of her mouth, and then all the way back to her jaw. Liquid silver dripped from the cracks, each seam bleeding more the longer she smiled.

She opened her mouth wider, and more of her face cracked

apart, and then she was screaming, the sound metallic and piercing.

The closer Isla came, the more of this girl there were, another copy, then another. And the more of them there were, the louder they screamed. Light blazed at the back of their glittering throats, the glow as fiery as if they'd each swallowed a meteor.

With her next step forward, Isla could feel the heat coming from the reflected girls' throats.

Slashes crossed their faces, the forms of other jewels etched over their own facets. Paz had scratched different cuts of stones into the glass as though the mirrored walls of the workshop were a sketchbook.

A panel of darkness moved, revealing a curtain of blazing light.

The light wavered at the edges, like the horizon buckling on a hot day. The screaming ricocheted between a piercing whine and a dull, rumbling noise.

Understanding struck Isla and made all the noise louder.

The screaming was the shrieking of the flywheels. The workshop was breathing out heat and light. And inside, Paz's silhouette drifted against the blaze.

FORTY-NINE

ISLA RAN IN, CALLING Paz's name.

Half the tables were on fire. The noise of the lapidary wheels was so loud Isla couldn't hear herself think.

But Paz showed no sign of fear or panic, no sign of wanting to or even being willing to move.

She just stood in the middle of the floor, looking as undaunted as she had standing on the roof.

Isla grabbed one of the buckets of water Paz kept near the machinery. She threw it on one of the flaming tables. The fire hissed, sputtering off steam and smoke as it went out.

But that left the rest of them.

"Have I ever told you about the Tavernier Blue?" Paz asked.

"Have I ever told you to shut up?" Isla's yell joined the

shriek of the lapidary wheels as she threw another bucket of grainy water over another table, then another.

Then they were out of water, and everything was too loud to let Isla think. The cracking sound of the flames. Paz just standing there going on about a blue diamond from hundreds of years ago. And worst, the earsplitting, brain-breaking scream of the machinery.

Isla grabbed a mallet off a table and smashed it into a flywheel. It spun against the ground and skittered to a stop.

Paz shuddered. Her eyes came to life. Their dark brown reflected the flames, and horror leapt over her face.

She understood now. She actually saw what was happening. Isla could grab her and pull her out of here.

But before Isla's hand reached Paz's arm, Paz darted out of the way.

"I swear I will leave you here," Isla screamed.

Now that Paz had woken up, she moved faster than the fire. She grabbed a bucket that Isla knew didn't have water in it. When she heaved it, a spray of sand flew out over a flaming table. She did the same with another bucket of finer sand, stopping the fire from jumping to the wall.

"Grab those." Paz nodded toward dust-coated canisters of fine grit.

They kept throwing them until the fire was out. They poured it all out until they couldn't see any live embers and the air was filled with the same grit that was hard enough to polish jewels.

FIFTY

THE SMOKE HAD BILLOWED through the open door and into the night.

There was nothing but tables and tools crumbling into ash.

Paz was coming back to herself, looking around in horror at the scorched workshop.

"I don't know how I could do this," she said.

The ash in the air was bitter on the back of Isla's throat. "You started it?"

"No," Paz said. "But I didn't stop it."

She had the same look Isla must have had when she woke up to the broken tile.

"A candle fell over," Paz said. "It's happened before. It's why I keep the water buckets close. I just didn't use them.

I just"—she stared at the singed walls, the disintegrating tables—"I let it catch. I let it burn."

Her shirt and trousers were wrinkled and lank with sweat, dusted with ash and soot. She was all pallor and dark eyes, and that spill of black hair that had come loose.

Isla thought Paz had looked destroyed when she'd taken the sapphire off her neck. But *this* was destroyed. This was regret hollowing her out. Paz had watched everything she'd worked for burning, and had stood back to watch it happen. Now she didn't even recognize the version of herself that had done it.

If she let Paz keep standing here, surveying the destruction around them, Paz would slip down into the dark. She'd be as lost to herself as she was when she let the fire spread.

Isla needed Paz to be Paz again, cynical and skeptical and far too amused about everything. Isla wanted to yell at her, *come back, come back,* the same way she'd wanted to yell at the open window Renata had left through. The same way she'd wanted to yell into the dark that Renata had vanished into. The same way she'd wanted to yell at Renata as she'd sat among the picnicking girls, pretty as sprays of flowers.

A flicker of orange made Isla turn toward one of the tables. Light breathed under a veil of ash, the dark orange of embers. Ash roiled and stirred around them like a new flame about to catch.

Paz caught her by the arm, stopping her. "They're not on fire." She plunged her fingers into the live ash.

A scream knocked into the back of Isla's throat.

But Paz just lifted her hand out. "See?" She held up a dark orange gem dusted in gray. "Just stones."

"Then why are they"—Isla couldn't think of another way to say it—"moving?"

Something flickered on in Paz's eyes, that confrontational spark.

"Blindfold me," Paz said.

"What?" Isla asked.

Paz was close enough that Isla could smell the smoke on her clothes. "Do you want me to answer your question or not?"

Isla untied the sash from around her dress. She set the light blue fabric against Paz's eyes and tied it behind her head, the ends trailing to her shoulders. So they wouldn't come loose, Isla fastened them in a neat bow.

Paz put the orange stone in Isla's hand. "Find a different stone that matches this in size and weight as closely as possible."

Isla looked back at the pile of rough orange gems. The stirring of ashes had slowed, but hadn't stopped. It looked like an enchantment spinning down.

She went from one table to the next, from magenta stones flecked with purple to dark blue ones set with white stars. None of them were stirring the grit and sand around them.

Isla chose a yellow-green peridot in a similar size, cut with similar facets. She set one stone in each of Paz's soot-grayed palms.

Paz walked to her right, confidently as if the blindfold had fallen away. She stopped just short of running into a burned-out worktable.

"The thing about tourmaline"—Paz ran her fingers along the table, tracing paths in the ashes—"is that it's slightly electrically charged."

She set both stones on the table. Smoky wisps jumped toward the tourmaline, but not the peridot.

Paz felt the space near both stones, feeling the grain of the air. "That means they attract ash." She held up the orange stone, wreathed in a cloud of gray.

A soft breath of a laugh laced the air. It was a sound of wonder that felt so outside of Isla that she didn't immediately place it as her own.

Paz had devoted herself to truly knowing beautiful things, not just gazing at them. She knew how to recognize an assembled stone or one that had been foiled. She knew how many facets were in each cut, how to check emeralds for injected oil, aquamarines to see if they'd been brightened with carbon paper.

"Your silence doesn't sound particularly impressed," Paz said.

This was a girl who knew how to hold rubies up to the sun at different times of day, to learn how they responded to light.

This was a girl who'd turned an unwanted stretch at a finishing school into a solitary apprenticeship as a gem cutter.

Paz didn't just saunter through the world to prove nothing could hurry her. She paused long enough to look at things, really look at them, rather than just find what was wrong with them. She went slow enough to see them.

Isla slid her hand onto the back of Paz's neck.

Even with the blindfold still on, Paz found Isla's lips with hers, smoothly and easily as telling one stone from another.

FIFTY-ONE

PAZ LEANED IN HER chair in that same casual way she usually did, like a young man just back from riding horses. As though they weren't in the Alarie House kitchen after lights-out, eating leftovers directly out of painted casserole dishes, their clothes grayed with ash.

"You never knew my sister," Isla said.

Paz took a swallow of water. "Correct."

"Then why mention her?" Isla asked.

"Why not?" Paz asked. "Everyone else does. She's one of those girls people don't shut up about here."

"Then why let me think you'd done something to her?" Isla asked.

"I didn't say I did. You assumed that."

"I didn't assume everything." Isla ate a slice of tomato directly off her knife, which no doubt violated fifteen rules of table etiquette. "You let me think you had control of this house. You more than let me think that. You told me that."

Paz stabbed her fork into a cazuela and left it there. "Yes, I did."

"Why?" Isla asked. "Why let me think that?"

Paz chose an apple from the fruit bowl. "Whenever I have an opportunity to make someone afraid of me, I take it."

"Why?" Isla asked.

"You know what I am. Who I am." Paz picked up a knife and sheared away a piece of the apple. "If people are scared of me, it's more likely they'll leave me alone. And when you're someone like me, you want to give people a reason to leave you alone."

Paz offered Isla a piece of apple.

"Letting you pare fruit for me," Isla said. "I heard I might as well invite you to put your head between my legs."

"A girl can dream, can't she?" Paz asked.

Isla took the apple piece. "Which one, you or me?"

Paz smiled and rested the arch of her boot on the lower rung of Isla's chair. She looked like a pirate king in a book illustration.

Isla unfastened the sapphire from around her own neck. "So if this isn't a stone to launch a thousand ships, why does it mean so much to you?"

"Why do you think?" Paz kept taking the apple apart, glancing up between flicks of the knife.

Her aunt, the lapidary.

So many questions Isla had asked, aloud or to herself, now seemed obvious. So many things were so clear now that Isla had enough threads to connect them.

Why do you think?

It was the answer to the question of why Paz loved the star sapphire as though it was part of her body.

Why do you think?

It was the answer to why Paz would readily make herself a villain. It was the safest role she knew how to take.

Why do you think?

It was the answer Isla probably would have gotten if she tried to take apart why Paz had let the workshop burn. The lapidary workshop represented the life Paz was not supposed to want. And the more that the air of the finishing school soaked into her lungs, the more she became at odds with that life. The kind of woman she was supposed to become was growing a life force of its own, and it was waging war on the woman she was and wanted to be.

Of course Paz would have wanted to wreck it all. Maybe only for one moment, but that moment would have been all it took. The second that candle fell and the first table caught, destroying the workshop might have seemed like the only way to quiet those two warring versions of herself.

In that moment, turning that forbidden world to ash might have seemed like the only way to let it go.

Isla tied the cord back around Paz's neck.

The knife paused on the apple. Paz shivered so faintly Isla might not have caught it if she wasn't this close. It was the same current through her body that Isla had felt when she pulled away the sash from Paz's eyes in the workshop. It had fluttered between them, brushing both their necks as it fell.

Isla was so unused to seeing Paz off her guard. She was all swagger and mystery, a girl in a man's suit with the face of a woman in a Waterhouse painting. She had the pointed chin, pronounced jawline, the slightly amused mouth. She was Circe on her throne. She was the obsidian-haired woman looking into a gazing globe, half sick of shadows. She could charm fish to the surface of a pond.

"So now you know everything about why I didn't want to be here." Paz cut the rest of the peel in a single green ribbon. "My question is, why did you?"

It would be so easy to say it had all been about Renata.

But the way Paz looked at her—nothing wry or smirking in her expression—pried something loose in Isla's chest. A star sapphire broke apart and turned into a constellation of white silk stars.

Then Isla thought of everything she'd have to explain. The differences in her anatomy, her hormones, the rhythms of what her body did and did not do. Organs that weren't there. Extra pieces of organs that shouldn't have been.

"I'm—" Where exactly was Isla supposed to start? She could go all the way back to when she was little, growing as fast as a boy, so quickly that people stared. *What are you feeding her?* they asked, as though Abuela was cultivating a rosebush. Then by eleven, she'd stopped growing entirely.

"The word people usually use is freemartin," Isla said.

She spoke the word fast, like a pinprick. Hearing it was one thing. Saying it herself was bitter as charcoal on the back of her tongue.

The word had once sounded like a mythical place in a story, until Isla learned it was a way to call out what she was.

"The exact definition I've heard is imperfect sterile calf," Isla said.

"I know what a freemartin is," Paz said. "You're not a cow."

The charcoal taste thickened on Isla's tongue. She had grown so used to being described in animal terms that sometimes she forgot she was being called a name for a calf and not a human girl.

"There are things about my body that aren't the way a girl is supposed to be," Isla said. "Or, I guess, the way most girls are."

She waited for it, for Paz to take a long, reappraising look at her body. She might start with a skeptical study of Isla's cleavage, augmented by lingerie Isla altered and padded herself. She was as good at it as an illusionist with his signature trick. But now Paz would see past it. She would see the truth of Isla, that she was a girl who had grown fast and then stopped growing at all, a girl whose body had started developing early and then stopped developing at all.

She would see that Isla was a girl frozen in amber.

"This probably won't be a great shock to you," Paz said, "but I don't have a very high opinion of anyone telling anyone how girls are supposed to be."

The words were a small thing, but they were enough. Paz was neither drilling into Isla, demanding to know more about the aberrations of her body and being, nor shying away from what Isla had just said. Paz gave Isla just enough space to explain the rest, the awful conclusions drawn, the assumptions that Isla was not only different but dangerous.

Rumors had decided she was the human version of an imperfect sterile calf, that like a freemartin, she must have had a brother. And because no brother stood before them, they decided she must have killed him.

"I never cared very much about being a certain kind of girl," Isla said. "I had enough trouble convincing people I was a girl at all."

Because her body wasn't what a girl's body was supposed to be, she must have done something awful. She must have murdered a brother she did not have, and then taken his cells, his blood, the molecules that made him. She must have stolen something to become what she was.

That was the story she'd been trying to get away from, that shadow brother. But the word *freemartin* tethered him to the truth of her body, and she could not get away from her own body, so she could not get away from him.

To the other children at school, she was a ghost story, a tale to tell in the dark. If she had killed her invisible brother, they could do anything to her, call her anything, and it would be nothing compared to what they assumed she had done.

"People are shits," Paz said.

Isla turned to look at her. "Excuse me?"

"You can dress it up with candlesticks and flower arrangements all you want," Paz said. "People in general have a spectacular capacity to be shits to each other."

As if summoned by vulgar language, a stately form appeared in the doorway.

FIFTY-TWO

WHEN AN ALARIE SISTER entered a room, the air shifted. It was like a spray of perfume, something rich and sharp, even before you could place which of the three had appeared.

In this case, it was Luisa. She hadn't even needed to enter the kitchen. She was merely in the doorway.

Isla straightened up, checking the distance of her chair from the kitchen table.

Paz didn't. She stayed in her boyish slouch, a finishing school sin on two counts.

Luisa looked both genuinely pleased to see Paz and skeptical that she was truly there.

"I heard you all missed me," Paz said.

Luisa gave the weary sigh she might give to a trouble-some but adored nephew. "Missing someone is different than worrying after them."

"Then I'm sorry I worried you." Paz gave her most charm-ing face of remorse.

This drew the closest to an eye roll Isla had ever seen from Luisa. "Get some sleep," Luisa said. "The both of you. Goodness knows I could use some. I'll need my strength now that you've returned." Luisa moved toward the hall.

Paz had come back. And that, apparently, was all the dis-cussion the matter warranted. They need not discuss the soot on Paz's and Isla's clothes, the graying of ash smudged on their faces and arms. They need not discuss the smell of smoke they'd brought in with them. They need not even discuss that two finishing school students were going about the uncouth habit of a midnight snack in the most garish way possible. If they addressed any of it—the soot, the forks directly in the casseroles—they'd have to address everything, and that would simply make matters unseemly for all.

The look on Paz's face reflected what Isla was thinking.

"Aren't you going to ask where I was?" Paz sounded delib-erately annoying. She had already known Luisa wouldn't.

"It's late, Paz." Luisa participated in the act, seeming appropriately annoyed.

But when Luisa kept going, something shifted in Paz's expression. It was no longer her wanting to irritate the eldest Alarie sister.

"I was busy playing with sharp objects," Paz said.

Luisa still vanished from the doorway.

Paz was on her feet now. "And setting things on fire."

"Paz," Isla said.

Paz took a few steps toward the doorway. "And engaging in astonishingly unladylike behavior," she called after Luisa.

Luisa's shadow vanished down the hall.

Paz's posture deflated. She put her hands in both of her pockets. It was a gesture that might have been meaningless on anyone else. But Isla had only ever seen her put one hand in one pocket, always like she was posing. That was a gesture of defiance. This was a gesture of defeat.

Luisa's discretion was so complete it left no room for Paz.

If Renata wanted Isla to let her go, Isla had to. But Isla wasn't letting all of this go, not for herself, not for Paz, not for Carina, not for all the girls in this house.

Isla saw her own hands grabbing at the gold in the walls. She didn't stop them.

In a second, Paz was at the wall with her. "What are you doing?"

Isla pried back the prongs of settings until one stone came loose, and then another.

The magic and madness of this place lived in the very walls. If they ever wanted the Alarie sisters to pay attention, they had to take it all apart.

But if breaking open the floor wasn't enough, ripping

jewels out of the walls wouldn't be either. It had to be worse. It had to be louder. It had to be something more shocking than anything they did after the Alarie sisters went to bed. And it had to happen in daylight. It had to be when they were all supposed to be in lessons or tutorials, so the Alarie sisters couldn't ignore it even if they wanted to.

Isla looked around the kitchen, the sheen of the copper pots reflecting her and Paz.

She lit the stove burners.

Paz swore under her breath, hands out like she was ready to stop her. "You just put a fire out. I'm not letting you start one."

"I'm not." Isla let her hands work from memory.

The artificial sugar melted into glass. It was so dim in the kitchen that it reflected the moon out the window.

"Do you want to tell me what you're doing?" Paz asked.

"Something they can't ignore," Isla said.

Paz watched her stir the dyes, check the candy thermometer.

Heat rushed off the sugar alcohol.

"How's your penmanship?" Isla asked.

"Overly masculine, according to Alba." Paz strolled toward the stove. "Crude, according to Luisa, brutish even. A rough imitation of round hand." She stopped two paces from Isla. "Lacking the flourishes of the Italian hand that is the predecessor of a modern young lady's proper cursive, according to Eduarda."

"But is it legible?" Isla asked.

Paz smiled. "Perfectly."

The sugar alcohol was bubbling like blown glass.

Isla turned off the burner. "Then get your ink and vellum ready."

FIFTY-THREE

PAZ LEFT PERFECTLY LETTERED notes under every girl's door, inviting them all to an early morning tea where they would eat sapphires and diamonds as though they were sweets. Paz and Isla left no way to reply, so there was no polite way to decline. The only courteous response would be to attend.

The girls came downstairs, the foyer washed blue from the predawn sky. They hesitated at the porcelain dishes full of bright jewels, cautious as if looking at something forbidden. Were they real? they asked each other. Had they come out of the walls? they wondered.

But then one girl said they were only candy, that they must be since they had been set out in candy dishes. When she put a princess-cut gem in her mouth to prove it, the rest followed. They set them on their tongues, reveling as though they were fine pastries. They weren't. The jewels were pretty but always had the dull, artificially sweet flatness of moldable sugar substitutes, the aftertaste only partly covered by fruit extracts.

The point was never the taste. The point was the impossibility of eating jewels. And for every candy gem, Isla and Paz had pried a matching stone out of the walls and hidden it.

Their little party began just as the sun was coming up. It would be in full swing by the time the Alarie sisters descended from the third floor.

Paz leaned against the hallway wall, looking on. She wore a suit that matched the darkest blue at the center of her sapphire.

She looked more dapper than any man Isla had ever seen dressed up. But her jacket was cut in a way so clearly feminine that men would have hated admitting she was their competition.

Her braid was loose enough that stray pieces haloed her face. Her shirt was buttoned low, that sapphire a blue planet against her skin. The white ruffle of a sleeve showed at each wrist of her jacket. She had the distracted confidence of someone who was striking not because of what she wore, but whose clothes were striking because she was the one wearing them.

The scene was perfection. The girls were conducting themselves as politely as if attending a wedding breakfast. But they looked like they were eating the Alarie House. They were finishing school girls with blue on their tongues as though they'd been drinking fountain pen ink, red on their teeth as though they'd been biting each other, purple on their lips as though the air in the house was freezing.

It was just the display with which to greet the Alarie sisters first thing in the morning, these proper, lovely young ladies devouring what made this place glitter.

Isla and Paz waited for creaking from the third-floor staircase.

But it stayed quiet.

Sun flooded through the windows.

And still the Alarie sisters didn't appear.

FIFTY-FOUR

IF THE GUESTS OF honor were late, Isla would go find them. She would come in running, so she was flushed and out of breath. She would let the words pour out of her in a frenzy.

Luisa would tell her to speak more slowly.

Alba would tell her to talk more clearly.

Eduarda would tell her to stop for a moment and breathe or no one was going to understand a word she said.

Isla would tell the Alarie sisters that hell had broken loose, and that it looked like pretty girls with a mineral glint between their teeth. It looked like refined young ladies eating precious stones right out of the walls, as though this place was a candy house in a fairy tale.

The third-floor hallway had the same carpets as the

second-floor halls, the same wallpaper as the Alarie sisters' office. But there was a stillness here thicker than anywhere else in the house.

The bedroom doors were ajar. They were more like the dorm rooms than Isla had imagined, just grander versions with wider replicas of the same beds, larger copies of the freestanding wardrobes. Rugs lay precisely aligned with the floorboards.

Eduarda's room was as messy as Carina's. Yellow dresses covered her bed like layers of melted butter.

Scribblings of wine-purple lipstick crossed Alba's mirror, a shade Isla had never seen on Alba. There was drawing after rough drawing of a girl's face, so generic that it didn't look like any real person. Each attempt was crossed out with burgundy slashes.

There was broken glass on Luisa's floor. The thin morning light showed a layer of dust frosting the pieces. The shards had been left on the floor long enough to collect dust.

All three beds were empty. Isla was about to go downstairs, to check the kitchen, the library, the lesson rooms, the dining room. Then she heard the laughter. It was so young and sounded so girlish that Isla couldn't believe it was the Alarie sisters.

Isla sat on one of the sills, holding on to the frame and leaning out the window to look.

They were up there, on the roof, in the white-gold light of the morning. They spun along the edges in broad daylight.

A creaking, groaning sound rose up through the floor. It vibrated through the walls and into the windowsill.

At first, Isla couldn't make out what it was over the Alarie sisters' laughing. But when she shut her eyes and tried to draw it out, she heard the pained twisting of metal. It sounded like the chandelier frame being wrenched apart, except that the chandelier hadn't been up since it had fallen with Carina in it.

Isla ran back downstairs, and found her classmates clawing at the walls. Their mouths were illuminated, gold dripping from their lips.

FIFTY-FIVE

ISLA HAD WANTED CHAOS. She had wanted pandemonium. But she had wanted it to be as much an illusion as the smoke in an amethyst. She'd wanted a believable forgery, like the candy jewels.

What she saw before her was as genuine as the rough stones Paz cut in the workshop.

Candy shards were strewn across the carpets, the different colors like broken stained glass. What remained of the clear candy diamonds lay in fragments. They had been smashed apart between teeth or trampled under running steps.

The finishing school girls were digging their fingers into the wallpaper. They were bending and breaking the settings that held the jewels. They were trying to tear the gems out of the walls.

Gold slicked the settings as though the metal was melting. Some girls were trying to bite the stones out instead of prying them out, and every attempt left more gold on their lips.

Paz went to one girl, then another, then another, trying to stop them. But each time, the girl screamed, her face blurring like phantom shapes in quartz.

Paz stepped back. Even at a distance, Isla recoiled. As they screamed, they vibrated like tuning forks. They trembled like glass about to break apart. They did not stop until Paz showed them her lifted palms and retreated.

They didn't seem to notice the gold on their mouths.

The sky outside clouded over. The windows filled with tarnished silver, flooding the house with faint, cold light.

Gold poured out of the broken settings. Slicks coated the girls' hands, liquid enough that it should have been burning them.

It streamed down the stairs toward the foyer. It crawled across the floor like a tide lapping in. Out the windows, it rained off the edges of the roof. It dripped from the trees, beading on the dark green like luminescent dew.

It collected in the sunken atrium. The middle of the foyer became a pond of honey and glittering silt.

As it filled, a patch of blue flashed in that small sea of gold. It looked so familiar that it drew Isla toward it. She waded in, and molten light spilled from one tiled step to the next.

Paz called her name. But it sounded as distant as the laughter on the roof.

Isla went deeper in. The molten light did not burn her. It was warm as it dyed her dress. The surface was lit up as though the sun was striking it, even though there was nothing but the dark pewter of clouds out the windows.

Isla lifted the flash of blue off the bright mirror of the surface. It looked just familiar enough for her to place it, the marquise-cut stone she'd almost stabbed Paz with. Yet it looked different. Altered. On one side, it was a clear, perfect sky blue. On the other, cracks and fissures paled the color. When Isla turned it over, it looked like one stone, and then another one entirely.

As she kept turning it over, her dim understanding brightened. It started as a glowing vein, and then it illuminated everything, like the fire lighting up an opal.

The most adored girls here were unnervingly pleasant during the day, in the presence of the Alarie sisters.

They were reckless at night, almost vicious with abandon, when there was no one else looking.

They managed themselves down to the gesture in the polite company of class or meals.

After lights-out, when there was no one to judge their comportment, they were feral, impulsive versions of themselves. The girls here kept their madness to late at night, so late that no respectable function would ever call for their presence.

And now Isla had provoked them. She had dragged that madness into daylight, and now nothing could stop it.

The Alarie House didn't just teach girls how to conduct themselves.

The Alarie House taught girls to divide themselves.

They were cleaving their beings into the parts they showed and the parts they kept in shadow. They pulled themselves into pieces and then sorted themselves accordingly. On one side, they put every quality that comprised a perfect young lady—attention to detail, charm, precision, lightness, an unlikely combination of effervescence and exactitude. And the other side of them was forced to hold everything else, everything that didn't fit. Fear. Impulse. Recklessness. Any wild instinct or improper inclination.

Who they were all depended on how the light struck them. It all depended on whose presence they were in, what expectations fell on them.

From one angle, they were flawless, polished to brilliance, shining in the space between carefree and meticulous.

From another, they were wild, delirious, brimming with fevered energies that had no place in the finishing school versions of themselves.

"Is something troubling you, Miss Soler?"

Isla followed Eduarda Alarie's voice.

She stood at the edge of the sunken atrium. The yellow at her throat lit up, looking as much like fire as the gold at her feet.

FIFTY-SIX

"**WHAT IS THIS HOUSE** doing to us?" Isla asked, every word choked. The lower half of Isla's dress was soaked, and so heavy that each step was slow. She was dragging her skirt behind her.

"Think of this house as a lapidary," Eduarda said, so calmly she seemed like a different woman than the Eduarda on the roof. "It shapes each girl into perfection. It's not always the smoothest of processes. But it results in brilliance."

More gold spilled over the steps down to the sunken atrium.

"Consider the kind of pressure that can transform ash," Eduarda said. "You can let it make you crumble, or you can allow it to transform you into a flawless diamond."

The gold flowed down the steps like a slow waterfall.

"There's magic in pressure," Eduarda said. "All these things we teach you, when to issue invitations, where to place the soup tureens, what to put in your hair, it's not simply to quiz you endlessly. It's not just for the sake of arbitrary rules."

Eduarda clasped her hands in front of her. "We need precision to make mysterious and incomprehensible beauty. Beauty seems random. It seems as though it occurs by chance. But it requires order."

Eduarda said it so gently it sounded like a kindness. Just as Renata had.

Order. Isla had blamed Paz for seeding that idea into Renata.

But Isla had the Alarie sisters to thank.

Perfection required order, and her body was too disordered for perfection to take hold. Her cells were inhospitable to the very essence of beauty. She'd known that, and yet to be reminded of it here, in this house where Renata had so completely moved on from her, struck deep as crazing in an opal.

If beauty required order, it could not live in Isla's body. And maybe this was why the Alarie House was spilling gold onto its floors, making even more of a scene than Isla had meant to orchestrate. Not because better Alarie girls than Isla were prying jewels out of the walls. Because the house could tell that Isla was not the tidy carbon atoms of a diamond.

It wouldn't matter how gracefully Isla placed napkins on her lap or how smoothly she made introductions at a party.

Isla was chaos. Nothing she learned would ever change it. There were some edges that nothing could polish away.

"Every jewel in this house represents a girl we've transformed into a sparkling treasure," Eduarda said. The stones at her throat looked like a necklace of embers. "They've married royalty. They've become First Ladies. They've had yachts and ocean liners named for them. They've lived in castles, châteaus, manors, estates, palaces. And they all came here with parts of themselves better concealed from the world. Once they learned that, once they knew the art form of hiding certain parts of themselves away, we sent them out into the world. And there they dazzle even more than the gems we've installed in their honor."

"No one can do that forever," Isla said. "What you want us to do, it's not sustainable. Dividing ourselves like that? No one can do that. Not for long."

"Oh?" Eduarda lifted her necklace away from her throat. "Can't they?"

She turned over the yellow stones.

Their reverse sides were splintered and saturated with flaws, like they'd been scratched up from the inside.

Appearing as smoothly as the girls in the mirrors, Alba and Luisa were next to Eduarda. Their skirts looked like tinted fog around their ankles. The stones lit their faces with the pale blue and lavender of glaciers.

They turned over their own necklaces. All the stones, the blue ones on Luisa, the violet on Alba, were paled with inclusions and feathering that dulled their color and shine. All those flaws had gathered on the unseen side of each jewel, like craters on the far side of the moon.

When they each let them fall back against their necks, it was as though the flaws had never been there. Perfect stones adorned their throats.

As the gold grew deeper, it not only reflected the dark silver out the windows. It carried flashes of color, like every shade of sea glass.

"Every girl can be perfected," Luisa said.

The lapping gold bore a streak of wet green toward Isla.

Isla drew it up. Gold spilled from her cupped hands and then beaded away, revealing an emerald rough. It was thick with feathery cracks and inclusions.

Disorder. The kind of chaos that could render a jewel worthless. This was the story of Isla's cells, her body, her being.

"We all have flaws," Alba said.

"We each have a side of ourself better kept in shadow," Eduarda said.

"The things we pride ourselves least on," Luisa said, "the things we'd prefer to keep to ourselves, we give them space. But we give them space away from those we wish to think the best of us."

Isla heard their voices, but she did not look up. Her eyes were catching on every knot, every needle, every cloud marring the emerald.

"There's no use denying that we all possess sides that simply aren't fit for the world to see," Alba said. "And yet they're part of us. So we make sure to keep them distinct from the face we show to polite company."

"Then we can show the world only our best," Eduarda said.

Isla turned the stone over.

Every flaw vanished. This emerald was smooth enough to look liquid. Even uncut, the color was deep and rich, glowing a wet green from the inside. It lit up bright as rain-soaked meadow grass.

"It's simply unrealistic to think we can show all of ourselves all the time," Alba said. "This way, we keep anything unseemly to ourselves."

Like the impulses inside them, held down so tight that they came out as girls walking on balcony railings.

Like the rage that built in their throats, everything they couldn't say turning as hot as the cores of stars.

Like the instinct to kiss a girl whose very presence, whose very appearance, was considered a confrontation.

Like the impulse to burn down that which you could not give up.

"And if you keep a part of yourself completely in shadow," Eduarda said, "the world can't have it. They can't even reach it. Because they don't know it's there. It's yours alone." Isla could hide everything she didn't want the world to touch.

"Don't you want to be flawless?" Luisa asked.

Steps grew louder, the sound of Paz's shoes moving from the carpeted stairs to the hard foyer floor. The soles of her boots slapped against the wet gold.

"Isla," Paz called out. "Don't listen to them."

Isla opened her mouth, growling like a fault yawning open in the earth. She was becoming a girl made only of precious metals and priceless minerals. The gold had already dyed her dress. Her hair was already gilt-edged, the ends dragging over the surface. If she stayed in here long enough, her flesh would become diamonds.

Paz pulled back.

The power of making Paz recoil was a charge through Isla's body. It was as intoxicating as just-poured champagne or expensive perfume.

Isla tilted her head back, more of her hair soaking with molten light. The weight of it drew her down until she was floating.

The most perfect version of her existed in this sea of gold.

Isla shut her eyes. She opened her hands, letting her body drift in this luminous sea. She stayed so long the sky darkened into blue, and she could see her, the diamond-bodied girl reflected in the window glass.

FIFTY-SEVEN

SHE WAS A SHEER silhouette, an apparition against the clouds. But she was so alive to Isla that they had the same body. Isla could feel her own flesh glittering. She was melting into the gold, becoming it. The world was all gilded.

A green moon appeared above her.

Isla tilted her head up.

The green moon hovered in the silver-blue. Its lower curve dripped gold. There were craters and lunar seas, and they made pale blemishes on the surface.

Isla did not understand how it was floating there until she saw who was holding it.

Paz was studying the flawed side of the emerald as if she thought it was a shame to be the only one admiring it.

Then Paz let it go. She set it adrift on the gold sea.

The light in the emerald breathed. A blue-green glow illuminated the flaws and feathers.

Something rushed back into Isla, that feeling of a star stone shattering deep inside her, breaking apart and then configuring into a new constellation.

Isla remembered the taste of Paz's sapphire, that salt and lemon. It blurred together with the taste of the candy gems she had made tonight, and had once made with Renata.

The feathers and needles in the emerald were already something outside her. They were already becoming something unfamiliar, the landscape of a distant moon. She was already becoming unknown to herself.

If she could become that unknown to herself, she could become that unknown to Abuela, to Renata, to Paz, to Carina, to anyone she loved. She had become so enchanted with the thought of becoming something else, being made of different substances than her own bones and her own blood, that she hadn't noticed these parts of her drifting away.

She had pulled herself into pieces before she ever came to the Alarie House, into the parts no one could know about and the parts acceptable to be known.

And the Alarie House was where she had learned to do it again.

This was how it would keep going. She would keep learning to pull herself apart.

This was how there would be nothing left of her.

This was how she wouldn't know the parts of herself she'd lost even if they tried to come back to her.

Her feet found the broken tile on the atrium floor, and she opened her hand. The green moon drifted into her cupped palm.

The slick of gold on her fingers didn't taste like honey. It was bitter as wine as she slid the emerald onto her tongue.

The shape changed in her mouth. It was wearing down, breaking apart, dissolving. It was tectonic plates crashing together. It was crystals and superheated water. It was secret caves of wild meadow green.

Le jardin, the imperfections in the emerald. They were the lush garden, the seaweed forest. They were the life in her, and they belonged with the rest of her.

When Isla looked up, Paz was crouching at the steps, drawing a sapphire into her hands. The beads of gold on the deep blue looked like tiny coins drifting up from underwater.

This was not a polished round cabochon like her necklace. The stone was raw, the color varying across the rough.

Paz turned it over once, examining the flaws and silk strands as though the sapphire was growing a thousand stars. Then she took those stars on her tongue, the flaws melting together with the perfect blue.

The other girls were no longer clawing at the wallpaper and prying stones out of their settings. They were watching. And a few at a time, they were coming downstairs. They were tracking flashes of color under the surface like comets. Their fingertips brushed the gold, and they flinched back, marveling at their gilded hands.

But then they reached for the color again.

Different stones cast different tints on their faces, from the bright pink of opuntia to the cobalt of wildflowers at night. When they put them in their mouths, Isla could see it flickering through their blood. It was clear as a blush on the floor beneath their steps. It turned their shadows to washes of red or violet. It sparked yellow green at the ends of their hair and the edges of their fingernails.

More girls came downstairs. Their demure nightgowns were apparitions against the dark foyer, the gold warming the white. These were the cautious ones, the ones who'd held back at first. Now they drifted through the house like luminous ghosts with gold-covered hands and gilt-stained dresses. They each held a different gem between their teeth, so all of them together looked like white light splitting into rainbows.

The Alarie sisters stood watching with the stillness of disbelief.

Isla expected rage on their faces. Or willful apathy. Maybe they could ignore even this out of existence.

Instead, they watched as though vaguely remembering something. Their expressions looked surprised, hopeful, fragile. It was a look halfway between waking up from a baffling dream, and encountering a lover not seen in years.

Before the house had done anything to Renata, to Carina, to Paz, it had done the same thing to the Alarie sisters. It had drawn the fire and lightning from the raw opals of their hearts. It had pulled out of them everything unbecoming to a proper young lady, and exiled it to one corner of their beings.

And then their family name had demanded they be examples to every girl who came after.

This tradition, this awful legacy of deciding which parts of a woman should be shown and which parts should be made invisible, lived in their bones.

They watched the girls dipping their hands into the gold. They watched them put the gems on their tongues, wearing them down in their mouths until the seam between each half dissolved.

The Alarie sisters did not issue corrections. They did not declare the ways in which this was all an affront to etiquette. They did not tell the girls to take hold of themselves, or proclaim such behavior to be unsuitable conduct for finishing school students.

In the next moment, the Alarie sisters were not just the Alarie sisters. They were Renata and Isla pressing their thumbs against their own necklaces until the settings gave. They were breaking apart their own jewelry in full view of polite company.

They clicked the center stones of their necklaces out of their white-gold frames.

The minerals looked brighter, Luisa's brilliant blue as artists' renderings of Neptune, Alba's purple as crocuses in the snow, Eduarda's like honey lit up in the sun. They stared at them as though they could see inside, as though each one held a terrifying but spectacular world.

When they held the stones to their lips, Isla could barely tell them apart from the rest of the girls, all of them letting the two sides of themselves blur together on their tongues.

FIFTY-EIGHT

THE GOLD RECEDED SLOWLY, like a sea tide. Shallow veils of it still lapped over the Alarie House floors. As it drew back, it left gems on the tiles and wood planks, like shells washed in by waves.

When the Alarie sisters left, it was with hands clasped, the last of their own jewels under their tongues.

Maybe it was the light behind them. Maybe it was the way their hair fell or how their arms intertwined like willow boughs.

But they looked like girls sneaking away from finishing school. They looked like ghosts of themselves in a way that made them look younger. It made them look free rather than haunted.

Isla had never asked how many generations of girls in their family had gone through this house. She wasn't even sure they knew. But there they went, the last Alarie sisters to be finishing school girls, abandoning the famous Alarie House.

FIFTY-NINE

ISLA KEPT TRYING TO guess which one was Carina's. Maybe this yellow diamond, or that pink sapphire, or this powder-blue topaz. But she couldn't know for sure, and all she could do was wait until Carina's bones had knitted enough for her to come back herself.

When Carina did return to the Alarie House, she came with eyes watchful as a sparrow hawk's.

She moved from room to room with light steps, and those light steps seemed tentative both with her healing body and with the fragile hope she'd put in these jeweled rooms.

She didn't look devastated to find that her life would not be as she wanted, a life in which she wore the Alarie girl designation like a sparkling ring. The name Alarie might no longer mean elegant travel, invitations to famous weddings, the society pages. The Alarie name would carry scandal now, as much for the girls who'd studied here as for the sisters who'd been born with it. The name Alarie would mean a hundred different rumors about what had happened here.

And yet, Carina's sad, tranquil smile was one of acceptance. Her heart still held the possibility that the whole world could be jewels, every filled bathtub an aquamarine, every sun a yellow diamond, her own veins streaming with rubies instead of red blood cells.

She looked at each stone she passed, until she found a pink tourmaline floating on a spill of gold.

As Carina turned it between her fingers, the jewel looked like a coin she was flipping. It was pale with inclusions on one side, bright and clear as fruit on the other.

She gave it one last look, put it on her tongue, and closed her eyes.

SIXTY

GIRLS CAME BACK, ONE at a time, or a few at a time because they could not bring themselves to walk in alone. At first they were young. Recent graduates. But then some came who were older, ones with soft lines around their eyes. A middle-aged mother who came with her recently graduated daughter, both of them Alarie girls. Ones with silver streaking their hair like tinsel and ones with meringue-white hair. Women old enough that they couldn't have been taught by Luisa, Alba, and Eduarda. Women who must have been taught by the Alarie sisters' mother and aunts and cousins, or the mothers and aunts and cousins before them.

Some took jewels out of the walls, placed them under

their tongues, and felt the parts of themselves they'd divided melting back together.

Some found theirs and hesitated. They wandered from room to room with the stones in their hands. They flickered through the house like light through a diamond.

Paz was ready, her stance as sure as a boy's and fierce as a girl's. She was rebuilding the workshop, clearing the ash, repairing the flywheels, opening the door in daylight. And each time a jewel was taken out of a wall, Paz made a dyed glass replica so precise, so skillfully shaped, that there was no telling it from the jewel it replaced.

That was the start of Paz's reputation as a lapidary, the fallen Alarie girl with sure enough hands that she could create a perfect forgery. That was the sterling irony of it. People wanted her to cut jewels for them even though she could hand them back a fake and they might never be the wiser.

For girls who came back but didn't quite know why they had, Isla set out candy jewels, so they could dissolve them in their mouths and imagine the feeling of taking back something lost.

Sometimes girls came in without a word, in that same sleepwalking haze with which they'd gathered along the upstairs railings. They moved through the house, eyes cast up as though observing paintings in a museum. With unhurried wonder, they considered each jewel, searching for ones that called up something forgotten.

But then there was another kind of girl who came, the kind who had never been enrolled. These were girls who came looking for lessons in the social graces, who had heard that something had happened at the famous Alarie House, and that things were in such chaos they might be allowed to approach the gates.

These girls seemed nervous, as though they might be interrupting or intruding. They wore the plain skirts of farmworkers' daughters, fine dust frosting the hems. Or they wore the too-showy dresses of new money, the kind that old-money families would dismiss as garish. They wanted to know if there was room for them now that they'd heard so many Alarie girls had run off.

Paz told them to go home, that there was no Alarie House anymore. But Carina stopped them from leaving.

She gathered them on the grass as the falling light turned the horizon to sherbet. The energy around her made the fabric blossoms on her dress seem alive.

The girls watched Carina with the rapture of an apparition. They listened as the sunset turned her curls to light and her skirt to an illuminated rose.

This was why Carina stayed, teaching lectures on the grass, holding the Alarie prestige that had been left behind like a sheen of gold dust.

When Isla was small, the parteras had told her that there were other girls like her. Girls whose bodies did not match what they were told girls' bodies were supposed to be, like silhouettes a little off from each other in a shadow play.

Isla hadn't quite believed the parteras. She thought they might be telling her this to make her feel less strange or less alone. But maybe they had been right. In the same way there were girls like Carina and girls like Paz, there were girls like Isla. And some of them might have even been Alarie girls. They might have been out there feeling the distance between what they were and what they were told they should have been. They were all bending their hearts and bodies and wills toward the shape of that ideal young lady, sharp as if she'd been cut out of paper.

They might have been like Isla, tearing themselves into pieces before they even arrived at the Alarie House. Then, within these walls, they would have learned to tear themselves apart again.

There were girls who might not know they could come back to themselves, because they had never been allowed to come home to themselves in the first place.

For them, Isla stayed.

SIXTY-ONE

WHEN THE GIRL IN the black velvet dress appeared on the roof, Isla didn't recognize her, not at first.

She sat on the tiles, the clay streaked with dried gold that grew faintly pink under the moonset. Her dress fluttered at the hem like the edges of a black zinnia.

"I know you came here for me," Isla said. "I'm sorry you thought you had to."

Renata shook her head. "I came here for you. I stayed for me."

Isla sat down on the tiles next to her.

"I wanted to believe it," Renata said. "I wanted to believe this could fix everything. Girls like Caroline saying that it didn't matter if we had money, that it was new and crass and so were we. Then when I got here, I thought, maybe I never even need to see the Caroline Beegans of the world ever again. Maybe this was all some dream I could live inside. Maybe instead of people like her trying to keep us out, I could keep them out. And as long as I was here, any part of myself I needed to lock away, it was as though it didn't even have to exist."

A jewel sat in Renata's palm. It was orange and cut round as the moon Renata was watching fall toward the hills.

It wasn't as though Isla had never heard the comments about the two of them and Abuela. Society mothers and daughters spoke of Abuela's newly made money as though it reeked of striving. They said that Renata and Isla would never pass for la plata heredada, that they wouldn't be mistaken for old money if they coated themselves in antique silver. But it had been distant noise to Isla, humming underneath every-thing else. When you were so used to being put down about one thing, it was harder to notice when you were put down about something else entirely.

Isla had been the lesser Soler sister, smaller in every way. But she and Renata were more alike than Isla had realized, each of them pushing back against something.

"I'm sorry I left you here," Isla said.

When Renata's hand moved, the outer facets of the gem flashed red and then almost purple. "I'm sorry I left you at all."

Renata turned it over. She didn't even look close to

putting it on her tongue. She didn't even look like she was considering it. She had the troubled demeanor of knowing something she didn't want to know.

"Some of the girls who've been here don't know how to reconcile who they are in the dark with who they are in daylight," Renata said. "But I don't know how to reconcile either one of them. I left you and Abuela. And for so long after, I barely felt anything." She examined each side of the jewel with the quiet horror of surveying her own bones. "If I put these different parts of me together, if I hold them both at the same time, then they're both me. The part of me who left you, and the part who thought nothing of leaving you."

Isla felt a kind of sadness for Renata so textured it seemed woven out of different strands. Sadness for Renata as she was in this moment. Sadness for the older sister who'd looked out for Isla, who'd led her by the hand into every room where there were girls Isla thought would tear her to pieces. It had taken work to do that. And until that first night at the Alarie House, Renata had never said a word about how much. Even if she had done it gladly, it had taken something out of her. When you were perpetually looking out for someone else, even someone you loved, you lost part of yourself.

Renata probably never thought she could tell Isla that. And if she felt even momentary resentment, she probably tamped it down, told herself she wasn't allowed to feel it, not toward her sister.

It became the part of herself she had to deny. And like

every part an Alarie girl had to deny, it took on its own life. It grew teeth and diamond-hard nails. It breathed. It raged.

It had needed space.

First, it had asked for it in a polite whisper.

Then it spoke more loudly, demanding it. And when it still didn't get it, it screamed.

Renata had been angry at Isla. Just not about what Isla had thought.

Isla closed Renata's fingers over the stone. Her sister didn't have to do anything with it now. But she could at least keep it. She could keep the parts of herself she wanted to seal inside glass. The parts that kept flashing into view like a stone turning different colors from different angles. They were hers. They belonged with her, even if all she wanted to do right now was pretend they weren't there.

Maybe Renata needed time when she wasn't forever looking over her shoulder, making sure her little sister hadn't fallen behind or gotten lost. She needed time without Isla as her hindering shadow.

This time, it would be Renata going home to Abuela's, and Isla staying here, both of them knowing where to find each other.

SIXTY-TWO

EVERYONE KNEW THE ALARIE girls. They were the girls who could hold satin napkins on their laps without them sliding to the floor. They replied, promptly, to every invitation they received, even if it was only to express their regret that they could not attend. They were the ones everyone watched, sparkling through a room like bubbles in champagne.

They were the girls who wrote letters with the points of diamonds. They held streams of gold in their hands.

They were the girls with the jewels in their mouths. If you caught them laughing at the right time, you might even see it, the sharp glint under their tongues. If they turned their heads toward the sun or the stars, there it was, the flash of their teeth breaking the light apart.

AUTHOR'S NOTE

Fiction set in the past sometimes lives in a kind of middle space, bridging the story's time and place with the time and place from which the author writes. Perhaps most relevant to *Flawless Girls*, I write from a time and place of having more access to information and terminology about my body than Isla would have about hers. Today, Isla might embrace the terms *intersex* or *differences of sex development* as a way to understand her own experience and to be in community with those like her.

Though my experience of gender is different from Isla's— Isla identifies solely as a girl; I identity as nonbinary—my range of gender experiences includes being a girl. Specifically, a Latina girl, like Isla. When expectations of femininity collide with expectations related to culture and race, the concept of what it means to be a girl, much less the right kind of girl, becomes even more complicated.

It gets complicated further still when our experiences of our own bodies exist outside of the anatomical binaries we're told are normal. My body didn't follow what's considered normal for the designation "female," and though my specific experience may be unusual, there are more of us than a lot of people realize.

Opening our shared understanding of anatomical sex leaves more room for more of us. The same way that opening our understanding of gender makes more space. The same way that opening our understanding of femininity—and masculinity—moves us closer to a world where we can all show up as we are and as who we are.

To everyone who's part of this work, whether coming from a place of your own experience or coming from the place of being an ally, thank you.

ACKNOWLEDGMENTS

There are many people who supported the process of writing this story and who transformed it into the book you're reading. Here, I'll name a few:

Kat Brzozowski, who knew the vision for this book before I could even fully describe it, and who guided me toward it with every draft.

Jean Feiwel, for making Feiwel & Friends a home for characters like Isla.

Abby Granata and Arn0 for this stunning cover, and Elizabeth Clark and Aurora Parlegreco for the gorgeous art direction at MCPG.

The teams at Feiwel & Friends and Macmillan Children's Publishing Group: Emily Settle, Tatiana Merced-Zarou, Liz Szabla, Rich Deas, Teresa Ferraiolo, Dawn Ryan, Kim Waymer,

Ilana Worrell, Kat Kopit, Celeste Cass, Lelia Mander, Kelley Frodel, Jessica White, Stacey Sakal, Kerianne Steinberg, Jon Yaged, Allison Verost, Jennifer Edwards, Molly Ellis, Melissa Zar, Nicole Schaefer, Jordin Streeter, Lauren Wengrovitz, Carlee Maurier, Samantha Fabbricatore, Leigh Ann Higgins, Jo Kirby, Alexei Esikoff, Mariel Dawson, Alyssa Mauren, Avia Perez, Dominique Jenkins, Gabriella Salpeter, Ebony Lane, Kristin Dulaney, Jordan Winch, Kaitlin Loss, Rachel Diebel, Foyinsi Adegbonmire, Asia Harden, Katy Robitzski, Amber Cortes, Amanda Barillas, Morgan Dubin, Rosanne Lauer, Morgan Rath, Mary Van Akin, Kelsey Marrujo, Holly West, Anna Roberto, Katie Quinn, Brittany Groves, Hana Tzou, Chantal Gersch, Sage Kiernan-Sherrow, Mindy Rosenkrantz; Talia Sherer, Elysse Villalobos, Grace Tyler, and Alexandra Quill of Macmillan Children's School & Library; and the many more who turn stories into books and help readers find them.

Wallieke Sutton, and everyone who gets the mail where it's going.

Heather Thomas and Melissa Wiese, for friendship, power, light, and laughter.

The fellow writers who were there during the drafting and many rounds of revision: Nova Ren Suma, Emily X.R. Pan, Anica Mrose Rissi, Aisha Saeed, Martha Brockenbrough, Dahlia Adler, Rebecca Kim Wells, Elana K. Arnold, A. J. Sass, Katie Patterson, Mallory Lass, and Mary Chadd.

Alexandra Villasante, for your wisdom about how we as Latinas define and redefine our femininity.

Hans Lindahl, for your insights on how Isla could fully claim her own story.

I.W. Gregorio, for opening doors with your writing and your voice.

Michael Bourret, for your guidance and support; Mike Whatnall, Lauren Abramo, Nataly Gruender, Andrew Dugan, Gracie Freeman-Lifschutz, and the DGB team.

Readers: for going with Isla to the Alarie House, and for giving stories space in your hearts. Thank you.